THE SPIDER:
THE SPIDER AND THE SLAVES OF HELL

THE MASTER OF MEN!

SPIDER®

THE SPIDER AND THE SLAVES OF HELL

By Grant Stockbridge

POPULAR PUBLICATIONS • 2023

CHAPTER 1
HELL'S WARNING

THE CAR wavered around the corner into Sutton Place through a red light. It lurched toward the curb, but at the last moment, swung away hesitantly. The driver swayed behind the wheel, his head rolling. The car drifted across the street at a long angle, bumped over the opposite curb and finally dropped its front wheels into the well of a cellar stairway.

The engine died and the car hung motionless. The driver's body was bowed over the wheel. Presently, while lights were springing up in the house against which the car had rammed, the driver stirred himself. The left hand door swung slowly out and, afterward, the man climbed laboriously to the pavement and stood sagging weakly against the car. He began to walk, feebly; somehow he forced his reeling body into a shuffling run. He kept a fist pressed hard into his side and his breath came raspingly, in a strangling wheeze. Dark drops spatted on the pavement.

It was an eternity before he reached the next corner, wavered around it. There was a high white wall there and he staggered along it, bracing a hand that left dark smears. He reached a pair of solid steel gates and his eyes peered blindly for a handle—for a signal bell. He attempted to cry out, but his voice was no more than a whisper.

"Wentworth!" he gasped. "Wentworth, in God's name…" A

tearing cough bowed him almost to the ground, but even while it convulsed him he continued to bang his knuckles futilely against the solid steel....

The squeal of sudden brakes came to his ears, faintly. Back on the street where his car had been wrecked, another machine now jerked to a halt. Three men spilled from its tonneau and ran toward the abandoned machine. Guns glinted in their fists and, presently, one pointed toward the dark trail of death upon the pavement.

The men began to run, swiftly. Their feet lifted echoes against the walls of the deserted street. The car loafed along beside them, stealthily....

Before those unfeeling gates the man had dropped to his knees. His up-reaching hands beat at the metal. The footsteps were nearing the corner and there was a sudden, ringing shout of discovery. A gunshot hammered along the street—and the steel gates slid apart, smoothly, without sound. A wild fusillade of bullets beat a tattoo on the metal, but the man crawled through the narrow opening and once more the gates were solid, impregnable.

Inside the gates, willing hands caught up the wounded fugitive and from the lighted doorway of a house, across the court, a man bounded toward the group.

"What is it?" he called sharply.

One of those who had lifted the wounded man turned a turbaned head. The light from the doorway showed his dark face, the bushy beard of a Sikh.

"A wounded man, *sahib*, who asks for you," the Sikh called. "He was pursued to the gates."

"Bring him in, Ram Singh."

"No, no," the wounded man's voice was a whisper. "There is no time. Wentworth. Wentworth...."

WENTWORTH REVEALED himself as a lithe, compactly built man with a lean, intent face. A silken dressing-gown was about his shoulders, but otherwise he was fully dressed. He bent over the victim, saw the bloodstains.

"Ram Singh, the emergency case, at once. Jackson, help me...."

Then he caught the pleading in the man's eyes. "No, no," came the tortured whisper. "I tell you, there is no time. I am finished. *He* is going to blow up your house. It is mined, and the explosion may come... any minute. They pursued me, and as soon as they report to *him*...."

Wentworth's servitor, who now supported the man's shoulders shook his head, and the light touched his broad, tight jaws, the jut of a strong nose. He wore a regulation chauffeur's uniform, but there was an odd military erectness to his shoulders, a soldier's efficiency in his movements. "Shall I follow them, sir?"

Wentworth shook his head. "No use, Jackson. They've gone." He was puzzled by this wounded man's presence, by something curiously familiar in his appearance. He bent lower.

"Tell me about it," he urged quietly.

"You won't believe me," the man gasped. "Listen, you saved

my life once. I'm a crook, sure, but…
but I can't stand what *he* is doing…."

"What *who* is doing?" Wentworth
asked softly.

The man's head rolled in terror,
"No man dares mention his name.
Those who do… *blow up*. But all this
doesn't matter. You've got to get out. Understand? *Get out before
your house is blown up!*" He panted.

Despite his own bewilderment and doubts, Wentworth felt
that the man was speaking the truth. His eyes combed swiftly
over the courtyard of the impregnable fortress he had built for
himself on filled-in land between two abandoned East River
piers. The strong walls were electrically defended and there were
secret exits. But mining… yes, it might be possible.

A thrill of fear jerked him to his feet. Nita was in the house…
Nita van Sloan, his fiancée. He could take no chances with her
safety, but moving her now would be almost impossible. She
had been wantonly crippled in Wentworth's last battle with
the Underworld,* her legs broken and twisted. The operation
to straighten them had been successful, but it would be weeks
before she could be freed from the casts and braces. Any movement now not only would delay her recovery for weeks, but
might result in her being permanently crippled!

"Jackson, the gate," he snapped. "If those men are still in

---

* NOTE: This was told in the story of the Spider's adventures, entitled "Rule
of the Monster Men."

the streets, try to wound one and get rid of the rest. We must have some verification. Ram Singh—" he turned as the Sikh hurried from the house with the case of first-aid equipment—"get down to the cellars and see if you can find any trace of mining. Turn on the electrical listening devices."

The man on the ground raised himself feebly, "Why can't you believe me?" he whimpered. "I risked my life... I gave my life to warn you, and you delay... At any moment, this place will go sky-high. Look, I'll tell you *his* name. Listen, it's...."

What happened then was a thing beyond belief. One instant, Wentworth was standing, gravely staring down at the wounded man, and the next... *the man blew up!* Even as his lips opened to give Wentworth the name of this man he furtively referred to as "he," his body jerked—and then the concussion of the blast hurled Wentworth flat upon the earth! Before him was nothing that could be called a man. There were ugly fragments and smears about the lips of a crater torn in the earth. That was all!

FOR A dazed instant, Wentworth lay stunned upon the ground. He was aware of the shouts of Ram Singh and Jackson, of their feet beating swiftly toward him. Wentworth believed that the explosion the man had foretold had occurred, yet, awful as it was, the thing seemed too slight to have come from a mine. God alone knew how it had struck! Suddenly Wentworth was on his feet, running for the doorway.

"Back!" he shouted. "Back to cover!"

A violent blast behind him sent Wentworth staggering into the cover of the entrance. Ram Singh whipped open the door of bullet-proof glass and Wentworth reeled into the hallway. Instantly, he blacked out the lights and there was a sudden gauntness to his lean-jawed face. He was white rimmed to the lips.

"We must abandon the house," he ordered crisply. "Ram Singh, get to the *missie sahib.* Tell her the house is mined and we must abandon it at once. The nurse will prepare to evacuate with her instantly."

Ram Singh flung a *"Han, sahib!"* back over his shoulder as he lunged toward the elevator. A door in the right wall of the hallway flung open and Jackson plunged out, having come by way of a covered passage from the wall.

"There was no one in the street, sir," he reported, "except two carloads of the police."

"The police?" Wentworth snapped. "What do they want?"

Jackson shook his head. "They didn't come to the gate, sir. They were throwing a cordon around the area. I am sure they are police. I saw Lieutenant Danglon, in uniform."

Wentworth swore harshly. Emergencies were no new thing to him, not even those in which the police and criminals had seemingly leagued together to destroy him. For years he had interposed his fighting strength and shrewd brain between the Underworld and the civilization it menaced. Sometimes, in his identity as Richard Wentworth, dabbler in amateur criminology, but more often in the guise of the grim avenger of the night whom he had created out of his fertile mind—the lone wolf of justice whom the police hunted and whom the Underworld feared as the Spider. Only Wentworth's few intimates knew his secrets—and it could have been no other way. For the police wanted the Spider on countless charges of murder, since his executions of criminals were necessarily outside the law. From the Spider, the Underworld wanted—vengeance!

"I will warn the police," Wentworth said crisply. "Get below and start the motor of the big cruiser in the secret dock. When you have done that, return and help to transport Miss Nita to the boat. We will delay for nothing else. The armament of the cruiser will have to suffice…."

Jackson saluted and bounded back through the doorway in the wall. When it had closed, there was no trace of it all except a seam in the rock facing. Wentworth stepped to a light bracket and flicked the light off and on in a peculiar rhythm. A small panel slid open. On a darkened screen, he could see immediately the street beyond the gates. It was as Jackson said, but now most of the men would have been hidden, were it not for the fact that Wentworth was seeing through an infra-red television set. He picked up a microphone, threw a switch, twisted a rheostat knob.

"Richard Wentworth speaking," he said quietly, and he could hear the reverberating echoes of his voice, magnified a thousand times and flung out into the street from a loudspeaker at the gates. "Lieutenant Danglon, I have just been warned that my house is completely mined and is about to be blown up. Withdraw your men to a safe distance or I shall not be responsible for the results."

He clicked off the circuit then and threw on another, clamped on a head-phone set. His lips compressed until they were completely bloodless and the lines of his jaws grew rigid. He could hear the swift tread of Jackson's feet along the tunnel floors beneath the house. But it was another, slighter sound that seemed to tighten a cold fist about his heart. It was faint, almost undistinguishable—even through his magnificent electrical listening device—but it was unmistakable, a deep, regular ticking. When that ticking ceased with a whirring click… the house would blow up! *It was a time-bomb!*

WENTWORTH WAITED for no more. He hurled himself toward the doors of the elevator, sent it swiftly upward. He was shaken and angered by the cruel fate of the man who had risked so much to warn him—frantic over what might happen to Nita. But his brain clicked on calmly and logically, analyzing this thing that had happened.

His plans for the getaway were already made. If they were in time… No question but that this attack upon himself manifested some new rising power in the Underworld. Ordinarily, he would have heard rumors of such a criminal giant as this nameless man, but he had been preoccupied with Nita and her recuperation. For a few weeks, he had relaxed his guard. Wentworth's lips twisted in a slight bitterness. The Spider's work called him again!

The puzzling feature of this situation was the presence of the police. There could be no connection between them and the wounded man, and the very furtiveness with which they moved precluded any friendliness toward himself. There had, indeed, been an increasing hostility ever since his friend, Commissioner Stanley Kirkpatrick, had been ordered on a world cruise because of bad health. Kirkpatrick had suffered a heart attack which might be extremely grave. A physician and nurse were with him… No, Kirkpatrick would not even hear of this latest development!

The elevator clicked to a halt and Wentworth bounded along

"Give it the gas, Jackson!" he
shouted, as a headlight from a police
launch slashed across the deck.

the hallway toward Nita's room. He flung his robe into a room, caught up a coat and thrust a pair of automatics into his pockets. There was a furiously efficient haste in his every movement and the pulse in his throat seemed to have taken on the rhythm of that clicking infernal machine below the house... Yet, when he entered Nita's room, it was almost casually, with a smile on his lips.

The nurse was working over her swiftly, and Nita's violet eyes flew to Wentworth's.

"Oh, Dick," she cried. "Is it true? Your marvelous house... mined?"

Wentworth moved toward her, still smiling. "It seems to be," he admitted. "Jackson will be here in a moment. Nurse, we will take the entire mattress. As soon as we are aboard the cruiser, you will re-rig these various pulleys. Ram Singh...."

Wentworth's quick ear had caught the beat of Jackson's feet hurrying along the hall. He stepped to the head of the bed and gripped the mattress. His voice crackled with authority.

"Nurse, follow with those pulleys. Ram Singh, you and Jackson will carry the foot together. Don't worry, dear, I'm sure we'll get out in time." His own words were a mockery in his ears, but he kept the smile on his lips.

Nita smiled back at him. "There is something new, then?" she asked mockingly. "Somebody evidently doesn't like us, Dick, and I think we're rather nice people, don't you?"

Wentworth nodded and set his shoulders. The mattress, with Nita upon it, moved toward the door. The nurse stumbled along with the accoutrements. Her face was drawn and querulous with panic. She began to run....

"There's plenty of time," Wentworth said calmly.

Nita's eyes were fixedly on his face. Her lips formed soundless words, "You go, Dick. Go fast. Ram Singh and Jackson will take care of me."

Wentworth's heart seemed to swell within him. It was like Nita to suggest a thing like that. She knew that Wentworth put himself last when it was a matter of conflict with the Underworld, of protecting the people he loved from its inroads. She was saying to him now that, regardless of what happened to her, he must survive to fight on.

"Plenty of time," Wentworth muttered, but even in his own ears the sound was strained.

Jackson was fumbling with the elevator door. It had never stuck before, but it took a few seconds to open it. Seconds... Wentworth stood rigidly braced and kept the smile on his lips, his eyes on Nita's.

The nurse said, shrilly, "Can't you *hurry!*"

Jackson got the door open and stepped into the elevator with Ram Singh beside him, carrying the foot of the mattress. Even Ram Singh's graven cheeks seemed a little pale. The Sikh would charge single-handed upon a score of enemies, but this waiting for a mine to explode was shaking even his steel nerves. The elevator lurched downward and the wall drifted upward past them; drifted... The safety lock clicked in slow rhythm. The clock of the time bomb was faster, much faster....

"When we get into the tunnel," Wentworth said easily, "we'll try march-time. You count, Sergeant Jackson."

Jackson lifted a face that seemed to be all muscle and bone. They had served through a war together, Wentworth and Jackson, and death was an old enemy. He said, tautly, "Yes, Major."

"As soon as we reach the cruiser, get to your engines. Ram Singh take the wheel. I'll cast off." His words came out easily, deliberately slow. The nurse was making small gasping noises and he could see that Nita's slim white hands were twisted hard together to keep them still. "Just fifty feet along the tunnel," he said. He could hear his pulse again, feel it. Was it imagination, or could he hear, too, the clicking of the bomb?

Nita lifted a hand and set it on his own and there were small tremors running through her fingers. She said nothing more, only her eyes held steadily to his face, a slight smile on her lips. *"So long as we're together,"* said her eyes.

The elevator jerked to a halt and Wentworth's hand moved with swift efficiency to the catch, flung open the door. He stepped out. "Sergeant Jackson!"

Jackson began to time their pace, *"One,* two, three, four. *One,* two, three, four."

Swiftly, they swung along the underground corridor. The walls were heavy concrete and the floor beneath them was solid. Their feet beat out echoes that accompanied them like marching feet, and the nurse broke into a frantic run. Ahead now, they could see Wentworth's large cabin cruiser, under the lights of the boathouse. The faint purring of its powerful motor came to their ears clearly. Fifty feet, but even in the boathouse, a heavy blast could bring death. *"One,* two, three, four. *One,* two, three, four...."

Nita picked up the chant, turned it into a marching song. Wentworth lengthened out his strides. He was moving backward, the others forward. It would be faster that way, he thought. How much longer? God, there was no way to tell. Even the man who had brought warning did not know that. But his escape might bring the blast on ahead of time. Might… *"One,* two, three, four. *One,* two, three, four.…"

He heard the clatter as the nurse leaped to the deck of the cruiser. Wentworth knew an almost overwhelming impulse to break into a run, but it would hopelessly confuse their stride, actually slow them up. This was madness, running from death at a regulation army stride. The boat… Ah! Wentworth twisted about and found himself within a couple of strides. He stepped to the deck, eased down Nita's mattress.

"Jackson! Ram Singh!"

The two men jumped to the tasks Wentworth had assigned them. In three strides, Wentworth reached the last mooring and cast it loose, sprang to the switch which would fling wide the concealed doors beneath the abandoned pier.

"Give it the gas, Jackson!" he shouted.

The doors whipped aside, the motor's note deepened and the cruiser began to slide forward. Wentworth sprang to the deck. Another few seconds and they would be free, clear of the menace of the mined house; free to fight the rising new leader of the Underworld who could plot such a bold, frightful attack against Richard Wentworth. Another few seconds.…

A headlight slashed blindingly across the deck of the cruiser and, from dead ahead, a man's voice rang out:

"This is the police boat! Kill that motor and tie up at that pier. Hurry, before we open fire. Wentworth, we want you for murder!"

CHAPTER 2
HOLOCAUST!

WENTWORTH STARED incredulously at that blinding beam of light. *Wanted for murder…* the words whisked through his mind. No time to parley now. They must get away at once, or the blast… Yet they could not risk the gunfire of the police—not with Nita and the nurse in this exposed position.

With a sharp oath, Wentworth did the only thing possible. "Nita," he said, "so far as I know, there are no charges against you, or the others. If there are, I'll come for you. Good-bye. Jackson, full speed ahead!"

He leaped to the pier of the boat—house along which the boat was sliding, ran to the end where the police searchlight was strongest.

"Let the boat go," he cried. "Here I am."

The cruiser was rapidly gaining speed, water boiling under the counter where the screws lashed faster and faster. The police boat was angling in… but held its fire. They could see and recognize Wentworth and their business was with him. As Wentworth had calculated, they would not dare, under the circumstances, to fire on the cruiser. Wentworth let his hands drop as if in despair—as if surrendering to inevitable circumstances. The cruiser was almost clear, almost… The very air behind Wentworth seemed to beat off the slow measures of time. How long *now?*

Wentworth heard Nita cry out, heard her swift orders to Jackson and Ram Singh. She was too late. Nothing could stop the cruiser in time. The police boat was less than thirty feet away, coasting in with an idling motor. In a moment, it would be too late to do anything save surrender. Wentworth lounged toward the wall of the boat-house and his shoulder rested against a switch upon the wall. The stern of the cruiser was almost clear. Even as it moved toward open water, the boathouse doors began to slide swiftly shut.

Guns blasted from the police boat. The powder flame made long red tears in the night, jabbed accusing deadly fingers toward Wentworth. He shrank against the wall, felt the hot breath of the questing bullets... and then the closing doors interposed a shield of steel. Wentworth hesitated an instant to make sure that the cruiser would squeeze clear of the closing doors—then whirled and hurled himself madly back toward the mined house, and the imminent death from which he had successfully fled!

Madness? Yes, of course. He was risking his life to escape a murder charge whose nature he could not even guess. Yet it was more than that. He must be free to battle this new killer of the Underworld. Any sort of murder charge would lodge him behind prison bars for weeks, perhaps months. Meantime, this new menace which dared to herald its hegemony over the Underworld by an attack on Wentworth himself—on the Spider!—would gain strength day by day. No, he had no choice but to flee the police, and no place of retreat save this home which at any moment would be blasted into the skies by the explosives planted beneath its foundations!

Nevertheless, Wentworth had not acted without plan. There were three secret tunnels leading from his fortified home which he doubted that the enemy had either ferreted out or mined. If

17

he could gain those, there would be a measure of safety. But of course, beyond that, there was still the cordon of police....

Wentworth's mind raced with the swift padding of his speeding feet. He hurled himself into the elevator, jerked open a side panel of the switch-box and pressed a hidden-control button. Instantly, the seemingly solid floor of the shaft parted and the cage shot downward. Moments later, Wentworth plunged into a cement-lined tunnel that led northward and had its terminus in a shabby private garage where he kept a car. At its far end was a stairway, a trap-door. He must reach that before the blast let go; must, or... death!

An eternity seemed to beat past between each stride, each thud of his feet. The lighted corridor stretched off into infinity and the echoes of his stride seemed to him the accelerating clicks of that time-bomb sputtering to its final infernal climax. Madness to think that he would ever reach the trapdoor in time; complete madness. Thud... thud... thud. At last, the steps! He scrambled up. Now, quickly, the lever mechanism that released the trapdoor! Panting breath... pounding pulse.

The door opened upward but it crept, barely moved. Useless to press against it with his shoulder—you couldn't speed that mechanism. Silence in the corridor now. *Silence as the clicking of the bomb suddenly stopped....*

The lights blacked out and a great swing swept through the

corridor. The darkness moved against him in a solid wall. The breath sucked from his lungs; blood started to his nostrils. He knew the door had been brushed aside like a leaf; knew the violence of that hurricane puffing him upward. The darkness increased. It was in his own brain now. He was flying through air. He did not know when he fell to earth again....

LIFE STIRRED in Wentworth's breast finally and, after a long time had passed, he could see. Overhead, the stars were crisp and clear. It seemed a little strange to be able to see them so well, until he realized that nowhere was there any ceiling to blot them out. Wentworth rolled his aching head and saw the jagged outline of broken wooden beams, of piles of rubbish. Suddenly, remembrance of the catastrophe floated back into his brain and he pushed dazedly to his feet.

His body was one vast, numb ache and his clothing hung in tatters. Heavily, he turned his eyes toward his home and, unbidden, an oath crowded into his throat. Nothing that might be termed a building was left. His carefully planned and constructed home, with its art treasures of a dozen nations and civilizations, was... nothing.

There was a tumbled heap of masonry over a black crater in the earth. Even the mighty walls had been leveled. Wentworth turned away, began to drag himself through the debris. Police searchlights poured their blue-white glare toward the wreckage and men with hand-torches were beginning the search. The river... With an oath, Wentworth stared that way. No, the river, too, was empty. God, had the cruiser and police boat been hammered down beneath the black water by that blast? They had had time to escape if they had pushed on. Nita!

The shouting of the police came dimly to his ears. He remembered that he was wanted for murder....

Fumblingly, a scarecrow of a man in his torn clothing, with his shambling carriage and shocked brain, Wentworth picked a way to the street. The force of the blast had been incredible. Here, too, the walls of houses had collapsed. The street was littered with the bodies of men in police blue. They had ignored his warning. Death had struck them down. Ambulance internes were stumbling through the debris to recover them, seeking some trace of life. No one paid any heed to the stumbling, broken figure of Wentworth. He made his way heavily westward while his brain fought for clarity. These police deaths, too, would be laid at his door... Until he could prove his innocence, and smash the madman who had done this thing, Richard Wentworth must disappear!

There was no other answer!

"BLINKY" McQUADE

RICHARD WENTWORTH .

His very soul seemed to cry aloud for rest, and there was mad panic at the thought of Nita. He must find out... But for the Spider there could be no rest; no thought of self. This very night he must be upon the trail of the "nameless" man whom merely to mention meant frightful death!

Heavily, he recounted his few resources. Money... He had a few dollars in his pockets, no more. At two points in the city, he had shabby but powerful cars hidden in private garages and there he could secure guns and disguise. That was the whole of his armament and equipment. And he realized that he must go his way alone.

He could not drag Nita into that murder charge, whatever it might be. He could not allow her ever again to match her feeble strength against the ruthless brutality of the Underworld. She had suffered too terribly. Alone, penniless, without resource… Wentworth laughed curiously, his voice cracked and harsh. Why, that way, the Spider would be more dreaded than ever before! Richard Wentworth, and Richard Wentworth's pleasant, dilatory life, were ended!

The die was cast.

WENTWORTH SCUTTLED into the dark mouth of an alley and before the double-doors of a garage, he groped for a tiny notch in the bricks. Before this, he fluttered his hand in curious rhythm and the infrared ray, which emanated there, recorded the vibrations on a photo-electric cell. The doors opened silently.

Wentworth started in and then stopped, swearing softly. At the far end of the garage, a red light was glowing. It meant that this garage had been invaded since his own last visit! Wentworth stood motionless in the darkness, peering toward the red light. His lips were pulled out, long and thin. Only his intimates knew of this hide-away—Nita, Ram Singh and Jackson. Once he had brought Kirkpatrick here, but the commissioner of police was on the other side of the world now.

On silent feet, Wentworth stole into the garage. From a

compartment in the wall, he took out a tiny flashlight and let the beam play over the dusty car, over the garage itself. He smiled thinly as he saw that the dust on the handles of the hood was less thick than elsewhere. This new Underworld monster worked with explosives… Wentworth flicked up the hood and quickly found and detached the miniature bomb that was connected with the starter wires. There was a coldness in his chest. His unvarying precautions had saved him, but it was the fact that his cache had been found which turned him cold. Had he no secrets from this new criminal giant?

Wentworth knelt on the floor and manipulated the catches of a secret compartment there. It opened and he now crouched before a brightly illuminated mirror above a make-up tray.

A lotion turned his skin sallow and drew it tautly over the cheekbones, blotted out the lips completely so that his mouth was a lipless gash. Putty moulding turned his nose into a predatory beak. Except for the bushy black eyebrows he could assume in a moment, it was now the face of the Spider that stared coldly back at him from the mirror. But he was not through. Rubber plugs turned the nostrils into a wide, flaring blob; disks made his lips pendulous. Instead of drawing on the Spider's lank, black wig, he used gray grease deftly on his hair and became instantly an older, feebler man. From the recess in the floor, he drew out a pair of spectacles which had hoods attached above each lens. When he had put them on, there was no trace either of the Spider or of the dapper Richard Wentworth. He had become a half-blind itinerant safe-cracker known contemptuously in the Underworld as Blinky McQuade!

IT WAS close to midnight but the saloon was crowded. Blue strata of tobacco smoke undulated and the sour stench of beer made the air thick, but it was a strangely silent place. A few men slapped greasy cards upon one table, but for the most part they were silent and stared at their own frightened faces in the soaped mirror behind the bar. It was everywhere this way in the Underworld, these days. There was good profit, yes, from following *him*, but even the most brazen of the killers paled a little at the thing that had happened uptown. The radio was still blatting with it. Thirty-seven police killed.

And there was no doubt who had done it. *He* had said he would destroy Wentworth. The men in the saloon were not even talking about it. They were talking about everything else. But the radio kept blatting….

"The police knew that Wentworth was a dangerous criminal," said the announcer, "and accordingly took a large force to encircle his home. At latest reports, there were thirty-seven known dead, and seven still missing. District Attorney Wilton Foley had sworn to find and convict Wentworth and in this he will have the full support of Acting Commissioner of Police Sanford Dane…."

The door of the saloon pushed open and every eye swung that way, but it was only a stoop-shouldered man in a battered hat and shapeless clothing who peered about uncertainly through hooded spectacles. A man near the door suddenly laughed.

"Well, well, Blinky. Where'd you do your stretch this time? Podunk Center?"

Blinky McQuade snarled, "Go to hell," and shuffled toward the bar.

"Was it vagrancy or soliciting, Blinky?"

"Naw, it was obstructing traffic."

Blinky whirled toward his tormentors and his pendulous lower lip trembled a little. "Aw, layoff me, can't you, fellows?" he whined. "Geez, no wonder a guy stays away from this town."

"Sure, sure," soothed the bartender. "Everybody knows you're a great pete-man, Blinky. Whose crib did you crack this time?"

Their hooting laughter followed Blinky as he sidled to the bar and slapped down a half-dollar. They were glad of any relief, these men, and behind the hooded spectacles of Blinky McQuade, Wentworth's keen eyes swept the room. Their very noisiness showed their uneasiness. He had done well to come here. Definitely, they knew something about *"him."* What they knew, Blinky could learn. His attention riveted sharply on the radio, caught a familiar name.

"…Miss van Sloan seemed grief-stricken. She appears certain that Wentworth was killed in the explosion that destroyed his home. She is being held for questioning but District Attorney Toley admits he has no charges on which he can hold either her or the servants of Wentworth. Nevertheless, he ridiculed Miss van Sloan's story that the home was blown up by an Underworld enemy…."

Blinky nodded, an empty smile on his lips. "Saw that guy, Wentworth once," he said. "Put a bullet in him. He ran. Nobody needs to worry about a cheap punk like that. Underworld enemy—*phooey!*"

The bartender stared at him with an expression of strain and men sidled away. In the mirror, Wentworth caught their uneasy glances toward the door, and the darkness that led to the back of the building. Someone reached out and clicked off the radio and in the silence that followed, the scraping of one man's feet was ludicrously loud.

Wentworth felt happiness expand within him. True, his home had been destroyed, and there was a new menace rising in the Underworld, but Nita was safe. Alone, no longer tortured by fears for her, he could meet the challenge of this nameless leader.

Wentworth braced Blinky McQuade's stooped shoulders, which took inches off his normal height. It was plain that these men thought his boasting might bring reprisals from the new leader. That would be as good beginning as any... He started bragging again, and the words died off his lips, unuttered. Through the saloon had run a current of terror as perceptible as an electric shock. For a moment, Wentworth did not know the reason and then... he understood.

The thing he heard was beyond belief and yet, he could not doubt the testimony of his ears. Faintly, it echoed in from the streets, swelling, growing louder every moment. Lonely, desolate, there lifted—*the hunting cry of a wolf!* The howl lifted thinly, savage and ominous, was echoed an instant later.

A pack of wolves, running wild in New York's streets? Crazy laughter throbbed at Wentworth's throat. It was incredible, but was the destruction of his own home any less than that? That the sound had a specialized meaning to these men gathered here in the saloon, he knew without any question. Their stillness, their waiting, was death-like.

WENTWORTH TURNED toward the bar-keep and the man started as if awakening from a deep sleep. In a single stride the bartender had bounded over the counter. He stumbled in his anxiety to reach the door. He slammed it shut, bolted it and backed away slowly, fearfully.

Wentworth said, querulously, "Hey, what the hell? Did you hear a dog yapping? What's he scared of?"

The man next to him twisted a suddenly savage face. "Shut up, you fool!" he snapped. "*He* is on the way."

"*He?* What the hell are you talking about?"

The man aimed a vicious blow and, somehow, fumblingly, Blinky McQuade swayed from its path. After that, he grumbled into silence. A new sound was beating along the street— the swift, frantic running of a man. In an instant he was visible through the grimy windows of the saloon. A boy of about eighteen, he was sprinting straight toward the saloon doors. And the howling of the wolves was nearer....

The boy hurled himself at the doors of the saloon. He rattled and hammered and his face showed whitely through the glass. His eyes were strained wildly and his broken, pleading voice came through plainly.

"For God's sake, open the door," he begged. "Just open the door. They're after me. They're after me—*the Hounds of Hell!*"

The bar-keep whipped an automatic from his pocket and waved it threateningly. "Go away!" he shouted, and his voice broke. "Go away, you fool! Damn you—go, before I drill you!"

It was not the terror in the bar-keep's voice, nor the menace of the gun that made the boy flee. He twisted his head about and there was a sudden, louder howling of the wolves. He pushed out from the door and began to run on. His wail of terror came back.

Wentworth swore under his breath. Blinky McQuade could do nothing for that doomed boy, yet... the Spider must act! The terror of these men told more plainly than any words that these so-called "Hounds of Hell" were another manifestation of the new leader whom they feared. Where the hounds coursed, their master could not be far away!

Wentworth cried out hoarsely, in Blinky's voice, "Geez! I'm going to get away from here!"

He began to run wildly toward the blackened rear of the saloon. A man struck at him viciously, and he dodged the blow. Men, everywhere were leaping to their feet as his own cries spread panic. In an instant, there was a pounding rush of other feet. But Wentworth reached the doorway first. He knew his way perfectly, knew that the washroom window opened onto a narrow alleyway between buildings. Through the window, he hurled himself and began to sprint toward the street where he had left his car. The howling of the wolves, for such they must be, was loud and fearsome in his ears. From the sound, there must be a score of them!

It took Wentworth two minutes to reach his car and kick life into the motor, then he hurled it toward the street along which the howling of the wolves echoed and where the boy had fled. He whirled a corner and his brakes shrieked as he jerked to a halt. He had found the boy. Backed against a wall, ringed by three slinking, powerful gray forms, he was striking about him despairingly with a broom-stick snatched from a trash-can. Even as Wentworth jerked to a halt, one of the wolves sprang to the attack. Powerful jaws slashed at the boy's left arm. There was a cry, a spurt of blood, and the broomstick flailed out, hammered the wolf to the pavement.

Wentworth slammed open the door and, a heavy automatic in each fist, leaped to the pavement. A long leap and he had smashed a gun home against the skull of one of the savage beasts. Only one of them left now....

"Quick, into my car!" Wentworth snapped.

The boy wheeled about, the stick lifted defensively. A savage, blended howl poured down the street and around the corner loped the balance of the wolf-pack! In an instant, they were ringed in a semi-circle of death about the two men! Wentworth had deliberately held his fire. The first shot would bring the police and release them from the threat of these long, glistening fangs... but also it would bring examination of Blinky McQuade and his disguise might be pierced. Moreover, it would scare away whoever controlled these beasts. And that was contrary to the Spider's plans!

"Let me have the broomstick," Wentworth ordered shortly, and snatched it. Swiftly, he holstered one gun, poised the stick before him like a sword. "When I break the circle and order you," he said quietly, "make a break for my car. How bad is that arm of yours?"

The boy shook his head dumbly, clenching a fist about the fang-torn left arm. "For God's sake, use your guns and let's get

29

away from here," he whimpered. "One of *his* men is coming, and when he does...."

As if the boy's words had been a signal, one of the wolves lunged through the air toward Wentworth's throat. His powerful jaws were agape, slavering, the fangs ready... Wentworth's broomstick slid forward like a rapier. Unerringly, it drove between those ominous jaws. His arm locked, his whole body braced... and the lunge of the wolf did the rest. There was a strangled, whimpering howl of pain and the wolf dropped writhing to the pavement, its throat torn, its spine snapped at the neck.

Instantly, other wolves were tearing and snarling over the corpse, and Wentworth edged around the flanks of the feeding pack, drawing the boy with him.

"Get in the car," he ordered swiftly. "Drive to Holian Alley and wait there for me, I'll follow, as soon as...."

He broke off then, the broomstick poised in his hand. As if the whole pack were one animal, the heads of the wolves had lifted, sensitive nostrils questing on the air. One of the animals whined low in its throat, like a frightened puppy.

"Get in," Wentworth ordered softly, "and tell me why you were running...."

"God, I don't know," the boy gasped. "I was in a restaurant and I heard a man saying something about some phony ads for the Great Store. He said it would bring thousands of people to it."

"Some fake advertisements?" Wentworth asked blankly.

The boy nodded. "Then one of them noticed me and pulled

out a gun. I ran… and then these Hounds of Hell…" He broke off with a frightened cry.

The wolf pack whirled, suddenly, and was racing off frantically down the street as if death itself stalked at their heels. In an instant, it had vanished into the shadows, and around the corner stepped a man. At sight of him, the boy's cry became a shriek of terror. He flung himself behind the wheel and the car quivered with the violence of his start.

WENTWORTH STOOD his ground, staring in amazement at this man from whose presence a pack of slaughterous wolves fled, whose mere presence caused a man to scream and flee. And Wentworth was inclined to smile. The man was strolling, almost casually. He wore a derby hat and an old-fashioned black frock coat and there was a cane in his hand. He moved slowly, with a certain archaic dignity of manner and Wentworth knew, even before he caught the glint of silver in his hair from a corner street light, that the man was old.

Wentworth let the automatic in his left hand hang at his side and his grip upon the broom-stick rapier relaxed as he stood waiting for the man to approach him. If this was *his* representative, certainly *he* used curious emissaries. Wentworth watched the man draw nearer, still casually, still dignified, and then a little chill spurted up his back. A pack of wolves had fled the very scent of this man, and….

The shock of an explosion jerked at Wentworth's body. He spun around tautly. The red glow of the blast was still in the dark street down there where his coupé had, a moment ago, been carrying the boy to safety. Now his coupé was a shattered hulk

31

which collapsed, a smoking ruin, in the middle of the street. The top was a torn sheet of shredded metal. Of the boy, there was no sign or sound at all… The echo of the blast rolled off into the distance and, behind Wentworth, a man's voice spoke gently.

"Pray, sir," it said, "accept my compliments upon your truly valiant behavior. I was sure that, someday, Blinky McQuade would find the courage to fight."

Wentworth whipped about to stare into the long, seamed face, the blinking almost kindly eyes of the old man.

It was Blinky McQuade who answered the old man with a whine, while cold anger flashed behind the masking hooded spectacles. "Geez, boss," he said, "the lad was my buddy once. You can't pass up a pal when he's in a spot."

"Certainly, no gentleman could, Blinky McQuade," agreed the old man. "Still, it is passing strange in this modern world of ours."

Wentworth's mind was racing. Could this possibly be the leader of the Underworld from whom all the criminals shrank as from a mad dog? It seemed incredible, and yet Wentworth had before this known strange figures to rise to dominance of the Underworld. There could, at least, be no doubt that he was in some way connected with… with *him.*"

"Will you not," said the old man politely, "return with me to my humble dwelling? After your recent encounter, you will need refreshment. And there is always…."

Peering into the dark eyes, Wentworth thought he could detect the cold gleam of menace there as the man paused before concluding his sentence.

"Always," he finished, "the danger that the men who finished off your... pal might do the same for you! So I think, Blinky McQuade, it would be well for you to accompany me!"

CHAPTER 3
PAUSE FOR MURDER

THE HOUSE to which the old man—who presently introduced himself as Langdon Van Schlaick—led Wentworth was a narrow residence of brick jammed in between larger buildings and there were boxes of evergreen at the white-edged windows. The brass work about the door had an ancient polished sheen and Wentworth glanced uncertainly toward him. There could be no mistaking the fact that the man had threatened him, and yet this seemed a curious set-up for a criminal... for a murderer!

It was not that Wentworth, following the man with the humble shuffle of Blinky McQuade, was in any way intimidated by that threat. It was his desire to make close contact with the new criminal overlord—certainty that this curiously quiet man with his silvery hair was involved—that had caused him to bow before the veiled threat in the invitation to "refreshments." That, and an unwillingness to abandon the role of Blinky McQuade. There could be no question that such a man as Blinky would have acquiesced if for no other purpose than to spy out a home for future looting.

Van Schlaick opened the door with a latch-key and stepped aside with an old-fashioned courtesy to gesture Wentworth ahead. In the close hall, graced by an old-fashioned umbrella rack, Wentworth became aware of a curious scent of anise. For a moment he caught his breath sharply, suspecting gas. But the old man doddered in behind him and threw open the door to a parlor crowded with gimcracky Victorian furniture.

"I hope," Van Schlaick said gently, "that you will join me in a drink before you retire for the night. I can offer you a wide variety, fortunately."

Wentworth snuffled and dragged a sleeve across his face. "Well, now," he mumbled in Blinky's gruffly timid manner, "I've always wanted to try this absinthe stuff again. Ain't had none since I was in France. They caught me in the draft."

He saw a sharpness spring into the man's eyes behind the neat gold-rimmed spectacles and Wentworth kept an apologetic smile on his lips. Van Schlaick made no comment on his choice, but bent over a cellarette. Wentworth's eyes glanced over the room. He could not escape a sensation of overweening danger and yet there seemed no reason for fear. The man gave no outward sign of being other than he pretended, an eccentric well-to-do gentleman. And yet... the man had identified him by the name of Blinky McQuade, and the wolves had fled from him in terror!

Wentworth checked impatience at the man's deliberate movements. It was barely possible that he was wasting time here. That boy who had been blown up by *"his"* powerful explosives had stumbled on something—that much was obvious. But in heaven's name, what danger could a fake advertisement for the Great Store portend? He accepted the drink of greenish

liquor which Van Schla-
ick held out and made
his hand tremble a little,
as if with eagerness.

"I am going to invite
you," said the old man
gently, "to spend the
night here, Blinky
McQuade. As I pointed
out, there is… danger in
the streets."

Wentworth fumbled off the battered hat of Blinky McQuade,
and the hand that held the drink trembled still more. "Geez,
boss," he whined, "there ain't no need for you to threaten me. I'm
a right guy, I am. I'd like to sign up with the big time. Listen, I
can crack a safe like nobody's biz, and…."

Van Schlaick stiffened. "I have no concern with your criminal
activities, sir," he said. "I am rewarding your heroism in defend-
ing that boy. If you wish to leave…."

Wentworth shook his head. "Geez, no, I don't want to go out.
Them wolves is one thing, but this business of blowing up! It
don't look so good to me. Honest."

"I concur," Van Schlaick murmured. "Your health!" He sipped
his liquor.

Wentworth tipped his to his lips and appeared to strangle. He
recovered and tossed back his head with the glass at his mouth…
but in the momentary delay, he had spilled the contents of his
glass into the crown of his hat.

"I will show you to your room, McQuade," Van Schlaick said. "I hope you will find it satisfactory. I can recommend the bed, certainly…" As he maundered on, he led the way down the narrow hall to a door and thrust it wide, with a gesture. "Make yourself right at home. In the morning, we will talk over… the future."

"Yes, sir," Wentworth mumbled. "I'd like to. You remember what I'm saying. I'm a good man in my line. Yes, sir." He stumbled over the doorsill, actually delaying his entrance while his eyes swept the room. He caught the dim lines of a tester bed draped in chintz, an old-fashioned chair… And the door slammed hard shut behind him!

APPARENTLY, THE door operated a light mechanism for instantly bright lights flared in the room and Wentworth saw that what had seemed to be the outline of pieces of furniture were cunningly contrived paintings on a wall that had a hard, smooth finish… as if it were, in reality, a plate of steel! These things Wentworth noticed while he clamored at the door in the frightened voice of Blinky McQuade. He told himself that Van Schlaick, whatever his connection with *him*, could not possibly suspect his real identity. At worst, he was exacting vengeance for the destruction of one of the wolves. Hence he was striking, not at the Spider, but at Blinky McQuade. He continued his pleading through long minutes but received no acknowledgment through the securely closed door, which was the only opening the room possessed.

After a while, he ceased his useless shouts. Huddled with his back against the wall, he surveyed his prison. Certainly, it could be no stronger had it been intended for the Spider himself! It was absolutely barren of any furnishings and the floor and ceiling, like the walls, were plates of steel! Presently, Wentworth composed himself to rest as best he might on the comfortless metal.

He told himself that it was possible that Van Schlaick was only recruiting a safe-cracker for service with *"him."* That was his deliberately conscious thought but he did not believe it. No, that feeling of overweening menace was too strong. There was a positive threat here, a threat to his life. But he could only wait until it developed. He set his hat, with its two ounces of absinthe, carefully on the floor beside him and composed himself to sleep. In fifteen minutes, in half an hour, he might be plunged into a hopeless battle for life. Meantime, he husbanded what strength was possible. It was his inordinate will which could compel his brain to sleep at such a time....

When Wentworth's eyes flicked open, the overhead light still blazed down upon him and, for a few seconds he did not know what had awakened him. Then, sharply, he realized that the wall behind him... *was moving!* With a single lithe movement, he bounded half across the room and his hands flashed beneath his breast to the holsters beneath his arms. An infuriated oath leaped to his lips. The holsters were empty! Incredible as it seemed, acute as was Wentworth's guard, even in sleep, someone had removed his weapons!

His eyes centered sharply on the wall, studying it. Yes, it moved upward. It continued to move upward, but no opening was revealed. By the heavens, he understood now! It was not that the wall was moving. The floor itself was sinking steadily, and the ceiling followed at the same set distance. The door already was half covered!

No question now of whether his captivity was hostile. No question but that his feeling of peril had been justified. He was being lowered into some trap! His mind was fully alert. He crossed and caught up his hat. There was still a small quantity of liquid in its crown and the odor of the absinthe was pungent and sweet in his nostrils. He smiled thinly. If it was his death the old man intended, he might get a surprise! He stood, calmly waiting, his eyes questing the side walls to determine from what source the attack would come.

It was in the back wall that he first detected the opening. He faced it, balanced on the balls of his feet, and watched it develop slowly—a low and narrow door covered with slats of steel. His eyes stabbed into the darkness beyond and a grim tightness emphasized the leanness of his jaw. He caught first the green glimmer of bestial eyes, then the stench of an animal den reached his nostrils. No mistaking the doom that had been planned for him. Even before he caught the savage, hungry throat-whine of the fierce beasts, he knew that Van Schlaick had thrown him to the wolves!

On the city street, with a gun in his hand, he had not feared them. A broom-stick, deftly used, had been a lethal weapon. Now, he had not even a club to oppose the savagery of these fanged destroyers! In two swift strides, Wentworth reached a position beside the grated opening. In the same instant, the floor ceased moving and he knew that the moment of battle was at

hand! From the whining eagerness of the wolves, he numbered
them at fully a dozen. They could
tear down a man and destroy him
in a few seconds, unless… Wentworth stared down at his hat and
there was a grim readiness in his
eyes.

He heard the rasp of metal, and
the grill gate of the wolves' den
swung open!

FOR A long moment after the last barrier was removed, nothing at all happened. Even the eager whining of the wolves was
stilled. Wentworth retreated a slow step toward a corner of the
room and, abruptly, a great dog wolf leaped through the opening.
In mid-jump, he swerved, bounded again and hurled himself
straight at Wentworth's throat! There was a rasping snarl in the
beast's chest. Powerful jaws were agape and white slaver wet
the inch-long fangs. His snarl was a signal. Through that door
poured a thick-pressed pack of other wolves!

Wentworth danced back from that first charge, drove a knotted and flashing fist to the side of the leader's throat. The wolf
was twisted aside in midair, hurled half across the width of the
room. Others were leaping to the attack. There could be no fighting them off. In another instant, they would drag Wentworth
to the floor and, afterward, there would be no hope at all. Yet
Wentworth kept his shoulders to the wall and fought grimly
until the last wolf had flashed in through that black opening. The

leader sprang again and his teeth gashed Wentworth's sleeve. A smaller beast slunk in toward Wentworth's legs. The others crouched in a ring barely a yard away, teeth grinning beneath snarling lips… and they were drawing closer, closer. When they all leaped together, it would mean the end!

Wentworth sucked in a slow, taut breath. It was the moment for which he had waited. He had to be sure that the last of the wolves had left the den to attack. He whipped the absinthe-soaked hat out from beneath his coat and sprang straight at the leader! The other wolves flinched back from his charge and Wentworth, crouching tautly, struck the leader across the nose with the hat! The animal let out a strangled howl, as if that hat had been searing flame, tucked its tail between its legs and scuttled across the room!

With a quick movement and a resurgent hope, Wentworth flicked the hat at the noses of the other wolves and they scattered before him, cringing, utterly terrified. Their whines were puppy cries now, and their menace was gone… for the moment! A great backward leap took Wentworth to the cage door. He flung the hat savagely into the faces of the nearest animals and, as they broke and ran, he whipped through the door into the den itself and slammed the grating savagely shut!

Wentworth instantly leaped across the width of the den toward where a faint light showed another grated doorway. Beyond it, he could make out a brick-lined corridor. His feet made no sound and, beside the exit, he crouched to listen. Voices murmured faintly nearby, but not too close… and the light was dim.

He peered through the grating and found, as he had hoped, that it was merely barred. No need to lock the door upon the wolves. They would not fear that a man could fight his way, unarmed, through that savage pack! Wentworth lifted the bar cautiously, and slipped out into the corridor.

Behind him, the wolves were raising a fierce howl, as he stole along the brick-lined corridor. He could make out that, beyond a heavy curtain, there were the cluttered shelves and cages of a pet shop and grim mirth moved his lips faintly. It was a clever cover for the noises and stench of a pack of wolves! He could hear the mutter of voices more clearly.

"… clever guy," a man mumbled. "Ought to take fifty thousand out of that store. And I gets my share, just like any of the others. Me, and I got a title. Keeper of the Hounds of Hell. How you like it?"

"Pretty swell," the other voice was lighter. "Yeah, pretty soft. All you got to do is keep them wolves locked in. But, Geez, if they ever got out!"

Wentworth was quite close to the curtain. He snarled his lips back from his teeth, and the sound that came from his throat was the hunger-whine of a wolf! He heard a chair slam to the floor and the sharp rasp of startled feet upon the floor. The deep-voiced man snarled out an oath and reached for a whip.

"Get back, you devil!" he shouted, and strode toward the curtained door!

Wentworth shrank back against the wall, heard the second man clatter across the floor and slam the outside door in flight. He nodded approval, but there was a cold flame in his eyes.

41

That mention of "the store" had snapped his memory back to the boy who had been murdered the night before. He had been killed because he overheard something about a fake advertisement for the Great Store, and now this… Plain enough that the criminals were planning to loot the store, but what was the purpose of the fake advertisement? Obviously, *"he"* had some reason for wanting thousands of people to flock to the store early, to jam the doors, the street, and… Wentworth strangled an oath that leaped to his lips. Had those thousands been summoned there… *to die?*

The thought lingered in Wentworth's mind, as the keeper of the wolves strode fearlessly through the curtained doorway and sent the curling lash of the whip cracking into the darkness. Wentworth knew that *"he"* was utterly ruthless and, before this, criminals had used wanton slaughter to cover their retreat, to confuse the police and prevent pursuit!

EVEN AS the thought flashed across Wentworth's mind, his hands reached out, lightning-swift, and clamped about the throat of the keeper. He flung his weight upon the man's back and bore him, struggling, to the floor. His knees gouged into the man's back and the grip of his hands clamped down on certain nerve centers. The man flopped as futilely as a fish on land and Wentworth bent close to his ear.

"Where are the bombs planted in the Great Store?" he asked softly.

The man was suddenly still under his hands, and Wentworth eased his grip a little so that the man could speak. He prodded the nerve centers painfully. "Come, come," he ordered, "talk—or die!"

The man writhed. His voice came out hoarsely. "Who are you?" he demanded. "You couldn't be that mug in the cell. Them wolves...."

Wentworth laughed softly. "If you live," he said, "I will allow you to tell Van Schlaick to be more careful hereafter about his use of perfumery about the house. It was simple enough, really. The wolves ran at the scent of Van Schlaick and his house smells of anise. I took a drink of absinthe... But you wouldn't know, would you, that one of the essential oils of absinthe is oil of anise? I tell you this, fool, so that you will know that I am making no empty threat. You will talk or I will throw you into that den of wolves... *without your clothes!* You see, fool, I know the secret. You have beaten those wolves, always with the scent of anise in their nostrils, until they shrink from the very odor. A simple thing known as a conditioned reflex. But, if your clothes are removed, the scent will no longer protect you. Now, will you talk?"

Wentworth could feel the trembling of his prisoner. "In God's name," the man panted. "In God's name, you can't do that. You *can't....*"

Wentworth bent closer. "You are a criminal, a potential murderer with your wolves, and I... *I am the Spider!*" His tightening hands cut short the man's squeal of terror. "Now talk. Where are the bombs and when will they explode?"

"I don't know," the man panted. "I swear to God, Spider, I

don't know! They're going to rob the store as soon as it opens and then...."

"And then," Wentworth's voice was hard as ringing steel, "they will blow up the store; murder hundreds, thousands of innocent people!"

A sudden thought struck him. The pet shop was open so that meant the Great Store, too, would be flinging wide its doors, ushering in the thousands who were soon to die! Fury lashed him at such cold-blooded slaughter. He swore harshly... and in his anger, his grip relaxed a trifle! In an instant, the man had writhed out from under him. Wentworth was flung violently sideways and his head struck the wall.

His senses reeling, Wentworth staggered to his feet, but the criminal was quicker. Already, his fist was snatching out a revolver from its holster beneath his arm. Wentworth took a staggering stride toward the man and blackness swarmed into his brain. He slipped and fell to his knees... and the keeper of the wolves leveled his revolver. The man laughed, harshly.

"So you're the Spider, are you, punk?" he snarled. *"Then take it!"*

In the close confines of the corridor, the revolver's blast was like dynamite.

CHAPTER 4
DEATH ADVERTISES

TEN THOUSAND human beings does not seem a great many in times when the unemployed are tallied by the million, and talk of hundreds of thousands under arms beneath a dozen battle-flags is commonplace—but they formed a considerable crowd in Thirty-fourth Street, these ten thousand for whom death had advertised.

Ten thousand!

Death waited....

Most of them were women and they filled the sidewalk, overflowed into the street and blocked it from building wall to wall before the Great Store. Their separate voices, their individual jostling, indignation and excitement, were not identifiable but formed a vast conglomerate like the mumble of a gargantua's bee swarm, like great surf behind a hill, like an army's guns muted by the miles. But there was no threat in their voices; they were vulnerable in their individual humanity... as *"he"* had foreseen.

These people had no individual movement. A disturbance on the fringes, like the arrival of the squad of mounted police, communicated itself as a ripple, as a wind-swaying of tree-tops. It was more dangerous. The massed pressure was tremendous and some women were brushed from their feet, had to fight a screaming way up from the menace of sharp heels and aggregate trampling weight. Behind locked doors, the manager of the Great Store was pale and there worry and excitement glistened in his eyes.

Beside him, the stocky, towering figure of the acting commissioner of police, Sanford Dane, seemed mountainously solid. His hat was knotted in a thick fist and his close-clipped hair, emphasizing the blocky conformation of his skull, underscored the rocky immobility of the man. His voice was like that, ponderous.

"What you tell me, Slager," he said, "seems impossible. Why

45

in the name of God should anybody else want to run advertisements for you? Suppose the prices are ridiculously low. It won't ruin you."

Slager's shaking of his head was jerky with strain. "Of course not. All those people. I can't explain it, but the fact is there. No one in the store authorized those ads. If I don't open the doors soon, they'll smash them down, and...."

He broke off, swearing nervously, as the musical clatter of broken glass heralded the crashing of a window by the huge pressure of that waiting crowd. Men in uniform ran toward the sound, and a white-coated doctor and nurse followed. They would have to work from inside. Impossible to force a way through those close-pressed ranks.

"Can't you disperse them?" Slager's voice rose a little.

Sanford Dane's frowning impassivity did not change. "I have five hundred men out there. If the crowd were men, perhaps. It would be risky. With women, impossible. Hysteria, in the mass. It would cost lives. Open your doors, Slager. We'll do what we can. If I could understand the reason for those advertisements...."

The men on Thirty-fifth Street understood well enough. They took a particular glee in that understanding. Here, there was a slighter backwash from the crowd and the loading platform where the delivery trucks were backed was completely clear. Men in brown uniforms moved purposefully about, but with all their loading, the piles of parcels on the platform did not diminish. The articles they were putting on the trucks came from

VAN SCHLAICK

within. Two men were staggering under heavy canvas bags, but there were grins on their faces.

"Geez, there must be fifty thousand apiece in these bags, Joe."

"Fifty, hell. A hundred. Maybe more."

"*He's* plenty smart—eh, Joe?"

"Plenty smart is right."

They tossed the bags into the back of a waiting truck and started to return to the interior. An oldish gentleman in a derby and a rusty black cutaway leaned on a cane at one end of the platform.

"One more load is all I can allow you, gentlemen," he said softly. "You will go in force. Five guards here. And keep your guns handy. In fact, it would not bother me particularly if you had to fire a few shots. But make them count, my gentlemen. Make them count!"

Appreciative grins touched the faces of the assembled men in their brown uniforms. They formed a compact group at the doors. The man called Joe spat for emphasis.

"I seen Commissioner Dane in there. Want I should pick him off, Chief?"

The old man shook his head. "Hardly necessary," he said equally, "unless he gets in your way. He can prove very valuable to us… and then there are the bombs."

The men shifted feet uneasily. "They won't go off too soon, boss?"

"Not too soon," the old man agreed.

" 'He' has given his promise. Besides, the doors have not yet been opened. Hurry, gentlemen."

He stalked away.

The men in brown filed in through the delivery doors, walking close together with their hands on their guns, and no one noticed them because their attention was all for the waiting crowd; no one important. It was true that an officious floor-walker spoke sharply, but Joe went to talk to him and the floor-walker did not have time to scream. He couldn't—with his skull crushed in. They were unhurried as they moved upward toward the money vaults where a number of officials and clerks had been… *removed*. They trusted *"him"* in the matter of the bombs. As for the rest, they had their guns. And the doors were not open yet.

Over by the front doors, Slager was saying, "I simply can't understand it."

"Whatever the reason was," Commissioner Dane said weightily, "we can't stop them now. It's too late. Better open the doors."

THERE WAS one man who understood, and one man who might have stopped them—but blocks away across the city, in a dark tunnel beneath an antiquated house, that man was fighting for his life. That first shot had missed the Spider only because the terror of his name and his history was working on the Keeper of the Hounds of Hell. After that first shot, the man backed away from Wentworth's abortive attempt to snatch the gun, and began to take more deliberate aim.

Rolling drunkenly on his knees, Wentworth strained his eyes through the darkness. His hands swept the floor for a weapon… and closed on the dog whip. It was a feeble thing with which to oppose the deadliness of that heavy revolver, but to Wentworth it was hope. His hand closed on the butt and, in the same instant he struck—simultaneously as the gun blasted once more and drove concussion painfully against his eardrums. The lash had flicked out and snapped, an instant before that shot—against the cheek of the gunman!

A cry of pain was torn from the man's lips and Wentworth lashed out again, this time more deliberately and with a different purpose. The slender length of leather curled out and twisted

LOPEZ •

• DANE

with savage violence about the man's gun wrist. The revolver was jerked from his hand and, as Wentworth threw his weight backward, the man was hurled face down upon the floor of the tunnel. There was a third, muffled, blast of the gun and the wolf-keeper's body jerked, his hands and feet scrabbling convulsively on the floor....

Wentworth swore softly as he flicked the whip free of its grip on the man's wrist. He had wanted the man alive for further questioning. Too late now to worry about that. He reeled to his feet, whipped the man over on his back and caught up the gun, bent to search his pockets for ammunition. Time was so short!

The man had lived long enough to confirm his shocked guess at the purpose of those false advertisements in the newspapers—at the carnage that *"he"* had prepared in Herald Square.

For an instant, Wentworth paused beside the corpse and, from his vest pocket, slipped a thin platinum cigarette lighter. He thumbed open the base, ground it down upon the forehead of the dead man. When he ran fleetly through the shop and burst into the quiet of the street, he left a memento behind... a warning to *"him"* that vengeance already was on his trail! For where he had pressed the lighter, a vermilion symbol glowed, a thing of tensed hairy legs and poison fangs—*the seal of the Spider!*

Wentworth reflected bitterly, as he darted afoot down the street, that now his last hideout had been destroyed. Now Blinky McQuade, as well as Wentworth and the Spider himself, would be hunted day and night by the Underworld. It did not matter. Blinky McQuade's life also was forfeit to the old crook who called himself by the archaic and respectable name of Langdon Van Schlaick!

As Wentworth ran, he hurriedly stuffed fresh cartridges into the emptied chambers of the revolver, then thrust the gun into his belt. The glasses of Blinky McQuade were tucked into his pocket and his fingers jerked loose the deforming plugs and rubber disks that had distorted his mouth and nostrils. It was a hawklike face, ruthless with the lipless gash of the mouth, that was revealed. It was a face that had spread abject terror through the Underworld—the face of the Spider!

Hatless, he flung about the corner, spotted a parked taxicab. He swung himself into the car.

"Herald Square!" he snapped. "Here's ten dollars... Make it fast!"

The driver snatched up the bill and, with only a cursory glance at Wentworth, hurled the cab into motion.

"What's up?" he called back cheerfully. "Damnedest crowd down there. Must be ten thousand or more. Cops everywhere, doing nothing."

Wentworth shook his head but did not answer. If Kirkpatrick had been in charge, he could easily obtain the cooperation of the police. A comparatively simple matter, then, to disperse the crowd. Ten thousand... God in heaven, if they were allowed to enter the Great Store, there would be ten thousand bereft homes in this city tonight! Already, in the destruction of his own home, he had felt the overwhelming power of the explosives that *"he"* used. And *"he"* would do a thorough job. That entire, block-long store would be smashed to fragments, spilled down upon the helpless crowd.

"Stop at that corner," Wentworth snapped. "Wait!"

WHEN THE cab jerked to a halt, Wentworth darted into a corner cigar store and flung into the telephone booth, then stood for a moment steadying his breathing before he put through a call. There was a chance, just a chance, that he might save those helpless people with police aid. He knew Sanford Dane well enough to attempt an imitation of his voice; well enough to know that if the Great Store had called and reported the fake advertisement, as it well might, Dane would have gone to the scene. He was the sort of man who preferred direct and personal activity.

"Milhauser," he ordered, imitating Dane's tones when his call reached headquarters. "Milhauser, and quickly! Send him in."

When Deputy Commissioner Milhauser answered, Wentworth began to push out rapid orders in Dane's voice. "Milhauser, Dane

speaking. There's a plot to blow up the Great Store and there are ten thousand people trying to get into the store. Rush all reserves here at once. Wait for nothing, but break up and disperse the crowd of people at all costs. Get help from the fire department, and for God's sake, *hurry!*"

He hung up without waiting confirmation from Milhauser. He could only hope that the deputy commissioner would accept the order at face value, would be too startled by the substance of the message to question whether it was Dane who had spoken. At least, it was the best Wentworth could do to acquire police help. If it failed… Wentworth hurled himself back into the cab, and it leaped from the curb without renewed orders from him.

"Try Thirty-fifth Street, the loading platform," he called to the driver. He caught a flying glimpse of a clock and his lips tightened with dread. Nine-forty, and the doors were due to open at half-past nine. How long would *'he'* wait to strike after those thousands had started to pour into the store? No way of telling but one thing was clear. Once those masses of human beings were swarming through the aisles, it would be almost impossible to get them out before hell let loose. Impossible... Wentworth's face tautened into harshly grim planes. It was a word the Spider did not recognize this side of death. But that was possible, too. Death was more than possible....

THE DOORS of the Great Store were open but, for moments after they had been flung wide, no one could squeeze through the narrow funnels. They had been waiting too long, too eagerly. Finally, the uniformed men stationed there began to attain some semblance of order. A steady stream of human beings began to flow inward... into the death trap! Excitement rippled through the waiting thousands and the whole mass began to press forward toward the doors. Screams popped up. There were some who fell and were trampled before they could arise again. Another window crashed inward under the pressure.

The escalators were instantly crowded; elevators, jammed to the doors, began to shuttle their scores to upper floors. Even inside, the people were forced to move tediously by half-steps. Their voices were so lifted, the volume so great that a flurry of shots from the loading exit was scarcely heard and totally unheeded save by a few nearest the spot. They saw a man, in the tattered clothing of a derelict, dart inward; they stared curiously as he raced off through the aisles... that was all.

And other thousands pressed toward the doors, funneled through the narrow openings. To their minds, there was no inse-curity in these familiar aisles. To them the weighty stories over-head constituted no menace. If the bombs were ticking out the last hours of their lives, they made no sound audible to their ears.

What they did hear presently, and uncomprehendingly, was the mounting wail of fire sirens in the streets. Even that made no impression until, within the building, too, alarm bells began to clang. Startled section managers and clerks stared, wide-eyed, at the bells. To them, those signals had meaning and they sprang into action throughout the eight stories of the building.

"That is a fire alarm, ladies," a section manager bustled along the aisles. "Fire alarm. Please walk, don't run, toward the nearest exit. There is plenty of time, but I must ask you to leave. Please walk, don't run toward the nearest exit."

His face was dead white. He knew how many people jammed against those doors outside. It was all very well to urge people to leave the store, but when they *couldn't,* when humanity locked the very exits....

"Please walk, don't run...."

The section manager knew the faintest touch of panic. It was his duty not to leave until his entire section had been cleared and, at home, Sarah, and the two babies... He stopped beside a young woman who held a child by the hand. Why would people bring babies to a place like this? A cute kid. Eyes like Junior's....

"Please, madam, you'll have to go. That is a fire alarm. Walk, don't run...."

After all, the building was fireproof... but those alarm bells kept clanging. It must be very serious. *Sarah...* He ran for three steps before he remembered his own warning. A note of pleading crept into his voice as he moved rapidly through his section.

The section manager stopped dead in his tracks and his mouth gaped open, but it was from a woman's lips that the scream rang

The Spider was deliberately precipitating a panic!

out. A child burst into a loud, frantic wail and a girl clerk jumped on a counter and began to run. Women ran in her wake and a part of the store was instantly cleared. Even while the section manager stared, with his mouth gaping, his eyes incredulous, he realized that his section was clearing. In moments, he, too, would be able to leave… but still he stared.

It was not an apparition that he beheld, but a man. A man in a long black cape, with a black hat pulled low over his eyes. He was bounding along the elevated top of the showcases between parallel counters. In one hand, he waved a heavy gun and from the other… from the other, dear God, there dangled a human head! Dappled with red, it was swinging jerkily by the man's grip upon the long, blonde hair!

The section manager turned and the cry that poured from his

lips was close to a scream. Before him, the aisle had emptied. There was shouting and screaming at the doors. Panic there. He bounded into the rear ranks of the mob. Out in the street, was the scream of fire equipment. He could hear men's voices bawling, shouting orders.

"Turn around! Face the other way! Make way there, for the people to come out. The building is on fire!"

FROM HIS perch on top the showcases, the figure in the cape was shouting wild nonsense. The cape was a long black raincoat snatched from the men's furnishings department. The head in his hand had come from the beauty salon and the red was the carmine of nail-polish, but he kept the head moving too swiftly for anyone to realize that. He waved the gun in the air, and shouted; danced a wildly fantastic imitation of the average person's conception of a lunatic. The gun blasted, two, three times and overhead lights burst and dropped their shattered glass noisily upon the floor.

Wentworth's face was pale under his make-up. He knew full well the danger of the thing he was doing. He was deliberately precipitating a panic, and the results in the street might be ghastly. But it was the only way to clear the store promptly, even with the fire alarm he had turned in, now clanging wildly through the building. If women were killed in the stampede, it was a small thing in comparison with the number who would perish terribly if they remained in this mined building.

"I'm a headhunter!" Wentworth chanted. "I like heads with long hair... with long golden hair!"

He swung the dummy head wildly through the air, blasted

out again with the gun. Women were running frantically down the escalators. The elevators were discharging their scores beside the street doors and Wentworth's dancing madness goaded them to greater speed. He heard a woman's cry lift clearly.

"The Spider!" she screamed. *"The Spider has gone crazy!"*

A grim smile twitched at Wentworth's lips. That was excellent. If only he could continue his inane dancing until the last of them was clear. If the police pushed their way in, he was finished. They would open fire on him immediately. He could not shoot back, even to save his own life. The Spider battled only the monsters of the Underworld. He would have to flee; to abandon his efforts. The fools might even permit women to remain behind.

Wentworth leaped to the floor and plunged toward the front of the store, still swinging the head, and chanting out his madness.

For a moment, he crouched in the protection of a counter to stuff fresh bullets into a gun. He noticed, with a frown knifing between his brows, that some of the cartridges he had taken from the body of the keeper of the hounds were marked with red. What that signified he did not know, but there was now no time to consider it. His revolver fully loaded once more, he bounded toward the front of the store. It was at that moment that he saw the men in brown uniforms.

IN A compact wedge, guns in hand, bags over their shoulders, they were coming down the main escalator. Women were fleeing ahead of them and choked screams sounded from above. As Wentworth glimpsed them, one of the men swung a gun savagely. A woman's hat flew from her head and sailed gently off into space, but the woman… The woman slugged across the moving railing of the stairway and, afterward, pitched head-first to the floor below! That much happened in the brief instant before Wentworth could jerk his revolver into line.

His lips, tautened by the make-up, pulled back from his locked teeth and fury blotted out everything save that group of men in brown. He did not need now the fact that men in those same uniforms had tried to stop him with bullets at the loading platform. At last, the Spider was face-to-face with the minions of the ruthless overlord whom the Underworld, whisperingly, fearfully called *"he."*

Wentworth's revolver fell into line and he squeezed off the first shot, without thought or conscious aim. He saw the leader of the looters jerk to the impact of his bullet. Then, on the moving stairway, there was an answering and overwhelming explosion. Before Wentworth's eyes, *the man was blown to bits!* Behind the leader, other men in brown were hurled flat upon the steps. Fragments of green currency fluttered through the air. On the moving stairway, nothing remained that could be called a man. There was a battered something that rolled and tumbled down the incline; something that had been a head. A pair of legs jerked and quivered on the steps… that was all!

For an instant, the shock of the thing that had happened froze Wentworth into immobility. Fresh, horrified screams burst from the few women who were left to flee in wild panic toward the doors. A man shouted a challenge in a hoarse, commanding voice. Then the men in brown were picking themselves up, flinging bullets wildly about the store.

Wentworth, with that same bitter smile on his lips, crouched on the cover of a counter. Explosions were bursting out all over the store. One jarred into the counter behind which he crouched and the counter was hurled in fragments; Wentworth himself tossed, half-stunned, against the showcase.

But his wits, and the meaning of his triumph did not desert him. Wentworth knew now the secret of those red-marked bullets, of the swift death that had overtaken the man who had brought the warning to his home; and of that boy who had fled in his car from the wolf-pack. This, then, was the weapon on which *"he"* depended to rule the Underworld and to ravage the city—explosive bullets!

Explosive bullets were not new in Wentworth's experience. In the world war, there had been Buckinghams for the airplane machine-guns, but they had been baby firecrackers compared to the force of these pellets of death. Manifestly, *"he"* had loaded them with some newly contrived explosive of incredible power, since the little that could be contained in a .45 caliber bullet was sufficient to blow a man to bits!

Deliberately, Wentworth lifted himself and once more threw his revolver into line. The men in brown were plunging down the steps. Even before Wentworth fired, one of them wilted, and another was hurled kicking, over the banister. That could have only one meaning: the police had entered the battle!

Wentworth shook his head, once more squeezed the trigger. Another of the men in brown was blasted into infinity. In rapid drumfire, Wentworth emptied his revolver and, on the steps, there were no more living men. It was a sickening shambles. Accustomed as he was to dealing death in his battles with the Underworld, Wentworth was shaken. But he still had a task to perform. Drunkenly, he reeled to his feet, sprang to a counter.

The door was jammed with men in blue uniforms: the police. Wentworth drew their attention to himself with a shout.

"Get out at once!" he called to them. "This whole building is mined! It is going to be blown up. Get out and clear away the crowd! *Heed the Spider's warning!*"

He shouted and the police whirled to face him. Even as his last words were pumped out, frantically, they opened fire. A hurricane of lead swept toward the Spider and he pitched down behind the counter.

"I got him!" a man yelled hoarsely. *"I got the Spider!"*

BEHIND THE counter, Wentworth reeled to his feet. His left hand was pressed hard into his side and pain and despair twisted his face. For once, the boast of the police was not wrong. One of them had... got the Spider! Bitterness twisted Wentworth's mouth. Because he had warned them; because he had sought to save their lives, the Spider had suffered a wound when the battle against this new monster of the Underworld was just beginning.

Yet, wounded as he was, he did not waver from his firm purpose. If they would not flee from the store at his warning, there still remained a way to lead them to safety. They would... *follow.*

Fighting the numbing shock of the bullet, Wentworth

began to stagger along the aisle. He plunged across an opening between two counters and bullets whined savagely past his head. The emptied store rang to the concussion of police guns. Wentworth clenched his teeth and flung himself into a sprint. The coat swinging from his shoulders fluttered and caught at the counters along which he raced. Its weight was intolerable and his legs functioned stiffly, without their usual superb coordination. He lifted a fumbling hand to loosen the coat... but refrained. No, they must be able to recognize him, or they would not follow him to safety.

He stumbled, almost pitched headlong, and that fact saved him for the fresh flight of bullets flew wide of their mark. The door to the loading platform was only a short distance ahead, but it might well prove impossible for the Spider. The violent effort of his flight was inducing heavy hemorrhage and his strength seemed to flow from him. His brain whirled dizzily, and there was a curious, dreamlike trance about the scene, about the pounding of his leaden feet. The sound came vaguely to his ears, as if it were some other person who ran; who raced beside him along the empty aisle of the store.

How long before the bombs beneath the store would let go? Obviously, the men in brown would have been allowed time to escape, but no more than that. To block pursuit, the explosion would have to follow fast upon the heels of their raid.

Wentworth was impersonal about his problem. His mind seemed to race beside his stumbling body, and the question, of whether he would reach the doors before another police bullet took him, seemed almost academic. The doors, the cape, his stumbling feet and the hammering echo of the police guns merged into a nightmare of sound and vision that had no connection with reality.

When a bullet slapped a hole through the glass door at his elbow, Wentworth scarcely noticed. He knew that, finally, he had released the coat about his shoulders and he saw the black vault of an open truck before him. He went through that, scrambled somehow into the driver's seat. He felt the vibration of the engine numbly and the truck swerved wildly as he jerked into gear.

His hands on the wheel had no feeling at all. He had consciously to look at them to know that they were operating the truck. Guns made vague, silly echoes behind him, and the shouts of men… But the police were out of the building. They would pursue him. *They would pursue him!*

A crystalline clarity descended upon Wentworth's mind. He had no way of telling how serious the wound in his side could be, but was certain that, unless he soon received treatment, hemorrhage alone could kill him. Handling the truck somehow with his right hand alone, he contrived a pad against the mouth of the wound, drew off his belt and used it to press the dressing violently tight. He could not afford to lose consciousness… not yet.

Laughter pumped at Wentworth's chest—crazy, light-headed laughter. Was this, then, the end of the Spider… to die under the guns of the police? He sagged forward over the wheel, felt the truck stagger under him and fought to keep it from leaving the street. He saw the plate-glass windows of shops burst outward in a thousand fragments, saw people sprawled on the sidewalks and realized that he could hear nothing; nothing at all. It was only after a while that he understood. The bombs in the Great Store had let go. What he had seen and felt were the effects of the concussion, even blocks away....

DRUNKENLY, WENTWORTH peered into the rear-vision mirror. The police cars were hammering on his trail without let-up. He caught the glint of a leveled gun, the brief stab of its flame. No chance that, in his present condition, he could elude pursuit! This might be the Spider's last hour! Grim purpose settled upon Wentworth, with that thought. If he was doomed, at least the men who had destroyed him should not escape unscathed. Old Van Schlaick, if that was his name, merited some attention!

Up to this moment, Wentworth had driven without any goal except a refuge. Now he spun a corner, headed southward, and thinly the wail of sirens began to come to his ears. Traffic ahead was disrupted and police sprang out to turn it aside from the course of pursuit. It was fortunate. Wentworth could not have dodged the heavy truck. He no longer had the strength. He swayed behind the wheel as he fled. He thought the bleeding had been stopped, but pain swept over him in agonizing heat waves.

Could he hold out... until he led the police to the home of Van Schlaick? To the den where the keeper of the wolves lay dead? If he could accomplish that much....

In a dream, Wentworth watched the streets swirl past him—the scattering traffic, the open, shouting mouths of the police.

Once a bullet starred the windshield close by his face, but he felt not even the sting of shattered glass. He did not know by what instinct he eventually whirled the heeling truck into the street whereon stood the narrow brick residence of Langdon Van Schlaick.

He lost control at the last and, as he pulled on the emergency brake, the truck bounced over the curb and rammed solidly into the front of the building. The impact tossed Wentworth toward the right-hand door and his hand found the fastening. His left hand gripped the revolver and he turned its muzzle upward, squeezed a bullet at the door.

The shock of the blast swept past him and the door swung, broken, from one hinge… Wentworth somehow found himself on his feet beside the truck. He reeled through that gaping doorway, even as the police sirened their way into the street. Wentworth kept a fist grinding into his side, kept his revolver ready. If Van Schlaick showed himself… Through the hallway, he reeled, and found a cellar stairway. Presently, he was picking himself up off the floor at its foot and he was in the corridor where he had fought the keeper of the wolves. He reeled on and sunlight slashed at his face.

He peered about him, hearing the shouts of the police behind. The street was empty, save for a huge transport truck parked at the curb, its side door swinging open. Wentworth's knees were loose beneath him, and there was no strength in his body. He went toward the unattended truck, bent almost double with weakness and fatigue. The gun trailed from his fingers, an intolerable weight. He did not know when he dropped it, nor how, in his weakness, he managed to clamber into the welcome darkness of the truck.

Men were shouting somewhere, but it made no difference. Nothing mattered now. He swooned in a delirium of pain and heard the truck door slam shut, heard the motor begin to throb. Then the motor noise grew to the proportions of a hurricane. What the hell, was he imagining another explosion? He....

Wentworth did not see red fire slash upward like a titan's sword through the red brick house he had just quitted; nor mark the flying bricks and debris that ripped through the air. He did not know that one of those fragments tore through the side of the truck and struck him on the head. Merciful darkness already engulfed him....

The truck swayed in that shock and then, in fright, the driver bore the accelerator to the floor and got out of town. If he were found there, the police would hold him for questioning and this load had to roll. He had to be in Albany by night; in Buffalo the next day. He could not wait.

It was the same reason that actuated this driver when, beyond Albany, he noticed the tear in the fabric of the truck and opened the door to look inside. He couldn't wait, and the man who had somehow crawled inside of his truck looked to be dead anyway. He tumbled Richard Wentworth into the ditch beside the road and drove on....

CHAPTER 5
WOMEN MUST WEEP

NITA VAN SLOAN wore the unrelieved black of deep mourning on the day when the doctor first skeptically assented to her attempt to walk. The dark dress set off the exquisite pallor of her face and throat, but even her assured poise could not mask the drawn and haggard look. A month had passed since there had been any news of Richard Wentworth. A month… and the last report had been the garbled newspaper story of a madman Spider in the Great Store—just before terrific explosions blew the building to flinders!

Nita had donned mourning before that to help convince the police that Dick actually had perished for she wished to halt the search for him. She had worn it joyously, since, helpless as she was, she might in this way still contrive to assist Dick. But as days dragged past without any fresh word, the black had become hateful to her, become a tangible weight upon her spirits. It taunted her with the knowledge that Dick might be… might be dead!

What could have happened to him that he made no cause against this new Underworld butcher who struck and struck again—now robbing a wholesale baker, now an armored car, and again smashing a bank to bits with his titan's explosives? The city was mad with fear! These things were preying upon her. There could be no solution until she, herself, could enter the fight—yet the doctor was skeptical of her ability to walk!

But she must!

With the doctor and Jackson giving help, Nita walked falteringly across the living-room of the quarters she had taken immediately after Dick's disappearance. Here she was protected by Jackson and by Wentworth's other faithful servitor, Ram Singh and the police spied on her day and night. Ram Singh was away now, keeping watch over the Spider's one remaining hidden garage with its shabby car. Ultimately, Wentworth would come to that garage. He would have to, if… if he were still alive!

"Splendid!" the doctor cried, and Nita realized he meant her walking. "I didn't think you were up to it! In a few weeks, you can try walking alone. Rest now."

Nita smiled a little and the expression on her soft, full lips was strangely reminiscent of the grimness of Wentworth's own.

"I can rest later," she said quietly. "And I'm walking alone… today."

IMPATIENTLY, SHE freed herself of their assisting hands and, with painful slowness, made her deliberate way across the room. Each foot had to be lifted and moved forward with an individual and concentrated effort but… she walked! She was halfway across the room when the front door opened silently and Ram Singh stepped into the room.

Nita's eyes flew to him, but he gravely shook his turbaned head. The strength seemed to leave Nita suddenly. She staggered and would have fallen save that Ram Singh leaped forward. There was gentleness in the touch of his powerful hands.

The doctor scolded, but Nita impatiently dismissed him and summoned Jackson and Ram Singh to a conference.

"Beginning tomorrow morning," she ordained quietly, "I

69

NITA VAN SLOAN •

shall take up the watch over the garage. That will free you two for active work."

Ram Singh's teeth flashed behind his thick beard and Jackson's broad-jawed face settled into harsher lines, but they did not attempt to dissuade her. This was the woman Richard Wentworth loved and her word was law.

"Our work?" Jackson questioned.

Nita nodded. "We dare not hunt for the master because we might only find him for the police! Furthermore, he does not want us with him or he would have enlisted our help. This may very well be because he does not want to involve us as accomplices in the Street murder case. Our course is clear. We must learn all the details of the charge against him—and destroy it!"

"There is no danger, Miss Nita, that we might interfere with the master's own plans?" Jackson was frowning, worried.

Nita shook her head gently. "When has he ever taken the time to defend himself when there was work for the Spider?"

The two men remained silent. If they doubted that Richard Wentworth still lived, they said nothing. Nita rapidly outlined what she knew of the case against Dick. A gangster named Fritz Street had been shot at the Club Angelic with a gun registered in Wentworth's name and left on the scene; Wentworth himself had been at the club with Nita and Commissioner Kirkpatrick a short while before the shooting occurred. As to motive, the police pointed to the often repeated charge that Wentworth and the Spider were one man—and that Fritz Street's name had been linked to the vice racket.

"You will find out if the state has witnesses, and who they are," Nita went on steadily. "In a week, I shall be able to walk well and we shall visit this Club Angelic. I'll take over the watch in the morning at the garage."

That was all.

NOTHING HAPPENED on Nita's watch during that long week; nothing that could be construed as indicating that Wentworth was alive. The Butcher, as Nita had come to call *"him"* in her own mind, blew down a small office building and there seemed to be no reason for it except wanton destruction of life. Jackson discovered that the chief witness against Wentworth was the manager of the Club Angelic, one Manuel Lopez, who swore that he had seen Wentworth enter the office where Street was murdered.

That was the way matters stood when Nita declared herself able to attend the Club Angelic with Jackson as escort. She could walk well, though not rapidly, and it was still a fatiguing ordeal. The doctor thought that in six months or so her muscles would have returned to their former strength. Nita laughed at that, but at the Club Angelic, she took no part in the superficial merriment of the place. Presently, she and Jackson would compel an interview with the manager, Lopez, but now they merely watched in the hope of discovering why Lopez should have lied.

However, Lopez kept well out of sight, and the floor show got under way.

Jackson leaned toward Nita. "There is a girl singer here," he said, "the feature entertainer. Lopez always introduces her, himself, I understand. She's next on the bill."

Nita nodded and there was an almost feverish brightness in her eyes. "When we see him," she said, "we will go to his office and wait for him to return." She drew her dress-bag toward her and was grateful for the weight of the compact automatic it contained.

Her eyes, widened, focused beyond the light in which a limber-legged youth was gyrating in a tap dance. She was groping within herself for some contact with Dick; always in tense moments before she had known a certain calm steadiness, as if Dick's spirit were with her, helping her. She groped for that reassurance now, and could not attain it. The failure frightened her. Oh, where could Dick be!

Jackson's whisper startled her. "Lopez isn't introducing the girl tonight!"

Nita turned her attention to the girl smiling in a brilliant spotlight that left the rest of the room in comparative darkness, caught the patter of the master of ceremonies as he introduced her. Lopez was in hiding then. Had he identified her and become frightened, Nita wondered. She rose steadily to her feet, hand clutching the bag with its automatic. The girl was chanting some foolish song in a deep rhythmic voice, smiling, swaying her arms. There was utterly no warning of the thing that happened. There was not even a scream. The song broke in mid-note and… *the girl's head exploded!*

There was a flash of fire, almost invisible in the brilliance of the spot, a rolling concussion and the girl's head simply vanished. Her body crouched under the blow, her white arms still outstretched, her white dress still billowing… but it was no longer white. The spot shone impassively down upon the tatters of the chiffon, on smears that glistened, dully red. The headless trunk hit the floor softly and, after that stunned moment of silence, there were screams, curiously disembodied in the darkness, and the crash of overturned tables, feet beating in panic toward the doors sounded like the scampering of giant—sized rats.

THESE THINGS had happened in a flicking instant of time and Nita forced her eyes shut on the horror, turned her head away to struggle against a faintness that struck through her like pain. Curiously, that violence seemed to touch only her body. Her brain was abnormally clear and her hesitant words were distinct in Jackson's ears.

"Lopez expected this," she said. "That is why he did not introduce her. We know now what these Butcher killings are all about. Take me to Lopez's office at once, swiftly."

Jackson's face, staring through the gloom, was a white blank. "Lopez's office? Excuse me, Miss Nita, we should get out of here fast. The police are only looking for an excuse to haul you in again."

"Lopez's office!" Nita repeated.

There was a sharpness of command in her voice, and Jackson offered his arm silently, steadied Nita as she pushed deliberately toward the hallway that led toward the club's business offices. The lights of the ballroom flared up and showed the thick-jammed ranks of people fighting to escape through the narrow exits. Nita scarcely heard their gabble of panic. Her face was pale, her eyes violet fire.

"You said you knew what caused this?" Jackson asked hurriedly.

Nita nodded, not looking at him, "This makes the fourth

time that the Butcher has blown up buildings or people without apparent motive. It is unreasonable to think he would be so spectacular about merely shutting dangerous mouths... and *Lopez knew this was coming!*"

"Then he had been threatened, warned..." Jackson broke off with an exclamation. "You mean these bombings, or whatever they are, are intended to make people pay extortion money!"

Nita said, softly, "I think so."

They were moving in the dimly lighted corridor close to Lopez's office door. "We will remember this for the master's information," she said, and tried to believe that she would see Dick again soon. The very emptiness within herself belied it. Oh, something was terribly wrong with Dick. Terribly... She forced herself to speak. "We are still trying to crack this murder frame-up against him. This will help us to prove that Lopez was intimidated into giving his testimony—if we *can* prove that this is extortion."

They were outside Lopez's door and Nita broke off, listening to a man speaking within, frantic pleading in his voice. Her handkerchief-covered hand went to the knob. Gripping the butt of her automatic, she swung the door open slightly. A thread of light shot out, laid a vivid bar across Nita's face and the somber blackness of her dress.

Lopez's words sounded clearly. "For God's sake, yes!" he was crying. "I'll pay! Call off your damned killers, Kirkpatrick, or I'll be ruined!"

It was full confirmation of her suspicions that she heard, but

Nita's ears were ringing only with the name Lopez had used in addressing the extortionist. Lopez had called him *Kirkpatrick!*

It was impossible that Lopez should be talking to Commissioner Kirkpatrick, of the police. Even if Stanley Kirkpatrick were not cruising on the other side of the world, she could never believe that he would be involved in a contemptible racket. He was Dick's warmest friend, a man of utmost honesty and integrity. Yet Kirkpatrick was a somewhat uncommon name. Aside from the commissioner himself, there was not one Kirkpatrick listed in the Manhattan phone book… Now Nita was remembering that it had been Kirkpatrick who had invited Dick to the Club Angelic the night that Fritz Street was murdered! This was a mystery which she must solve at once!

Nita gripped her automatic, whispered to Jackson. "Keep watch here at the door."

She thrust the door wide and went into Lopez's office behind her ready automatic!

BEHIND A broad desk, Manuel Lopez sprang to his feet with an oath. His full, swarthy cheeks were glistening with perspiration. He spread out his palms.

"You do not need to threaten me," he said violently. "I was just talking to the boss!"

Nita was aware of the stiffness of her legs beneath the drape of her black dress. It was a tautness that extended to all her body; readiness reflected in the unwavering gun in her fist, in the steady burning flame of her eyes. Apparently, Lopez had mistaken her for some ally of the extortionists, come to enforce their demands.

"I do not threaten," she said in a dead, level voice. "I kill. Call the boss again, and let me hear you tell him that. Call… Kirkpatrick!"

Lopez bent forward, fat hands flat on the desk. His body bobbed with the vehemence of his words. "But I am telling you. I already call him. Listen, I pay right away. Quick."

"Quit stalling," Nita instructed. "The girl lost her head, didn't she?" Her automatic's muzzle lifted an inch, and its black snout stared into Lopez's face. *Call Kirkpatrick!*"

Lopez dropped back into the chair, his face a dirty gray. His hands trembled as they groped for his telephone. Nita wondered a little at herself. She knew that she was capable of shooting if this man did not obey, and that fact had communicated itself to Lopez. It had something to do with the coldness that clustered about her heart; with the fact that she could no longer feel, in this crisis, the nearness of the man she loved….

She moved three slow steps nearer the desk and watched Lopez's hands as he began to dial. *M… U…* Nita held her breath. That was Murray Hill, the exchange in which Stanley Kirkpatrick's phone was listed. If the next digit were 7. She held her breath, eyes fixed unwaveringly on the man's hand, saw an over-manicured finger slip into the dial slot of the 7!

It was Nita's intense preoccupation with the number that Lopez was dialing which prevented her hearing movement just behind and to her right. When finally the sound penetrated her consciousness, she whipped the gun around—too late! Two hands clamped down on her right wrist and a foot kicked her right ankle violently out from under her!

The pain in her right ankle, so recently healed, brought a sharp cry from Nita. After that moment she uttered no sound, but began to fight fiercely. It was a woman who had seized her gun-wrist, a girl as dark and lithe as Lopez was fat. Her dark eyes were wide and blazing with hatred, and she threw her body's weight into the effort to wrest the gun from Nita.

Nita had sagged to her knees under the attack. Out of her eye corners, she saw Lopez slap open the drawer of the desk and knew that he was grabbing for a weapon. Nita's own coolness surprised her. She acted with calm efficiency, thankful that Dick long ago had insisted on her learning *jiu-jitsu*. It was the principle of that exact science which she employed now.

The girl was straining back with all her strength to wrest away the automatic. Nita let go of the gun and clamped her left hand about the girl's ankle. The girl's own violence did the rest. She tripped, pitched heavily to the floor. Her arms flew wide and the gun skittered across the floor toward the desk. On her knees, Nita threw herself toward the furious prostrate girl.

The stiffened fingers of her right hand darted like a sword-thrust to nerve-centers in the girl's exposed throat. They plunged home and the strangled cry, the convulsive jerk of muscles, told Nita that she had struck true. She was already rolling toward the desk, toward her gun, and for the first time could turn her attention back to Lopez. He was lifting a heavy gun from his drawer. So swift had been the attack and Nita's counter that he had had time for no more than that. Before he could bring the gun to bear upon her, Nita rolled hard up against the desk and her eager fingers closed about the butt of her automatic.

IT WAS at that same moment that the outer door of the office swished inward under the drive of Jackson's shoulder. His gun was ready in his fist and she caught the flash of his chill blue eyes as they swept over the room. She saw flame spit from the muzzle of his automatic, saw it kick upward against the stiffness of his wrist but somehow the blast of the shot made no impression on her senses.

Behind the desk, the chair creaked under a sharp, heavy strain. The gun clattered to the floor and afterward, slowly, two feet pushed forward across the thick green rug upon the floor. She saw the heels dig up the pile, then the knees bent and there was the softened thump of Lopez slumping out of the chair.

Nita climbed stiffly to her feet. "The girl must have seen the door open," she said clearly. "She hid close against the wall until my back was entirely turned to her."

Jackson said, "Excuse me, Miss Nita." He flung an arm about her waist, swung her from her feet and leaped toward the door.

"Wait!" Nita snapped. "Wait… the Spider always signs his justice."

Jackson was startled into stopping. Nita thrust clear and staggered back to the desk. She dipped her finger into black ink, and stooped to scrawl upon the white shirt front of dead Lopez, a silhouette of the Spider's seal.

"Black," she whispered as she ran awkwardly toward Jackson. *"Black!"* Her voice broke, rose thinly. "The Black Widow can sting, too, Jackson. *The Black Widow…."*

It was in that same moment that Nita realized she really believed Richard Wentworth was dead.

Jackson caught her up and plunged out into the dimness of the hall. He ran swiftly, head thrown back with violent effort, fist knotted hard about his automatic. Ahead, Nita saw men spring out of a doorway—men clad in the blue uniforms of the police.

"Halt!" the leader shouted. "Halt, or I'll fire!" Jackson pivoted into a doorway on the right and a gun sent its thunderous echo along the hall. Nita heard the heavy pound of running feet as Jackson bolted the door. She moved calmly toward the window. It had been madness to scrawl that Spider upon Lopez's chest. Even if the girl could not identify her later, they seemed inextricably trapped. Already, she could hear the police beating at the door, heard their leader shout an order to cover the window. She flung the window wide.

"It will have to be the roof, Jackson," she said quietly. "You have the Spider's web, as I instructed."

Jackson whipped a length of silken rope from about his waist, and there was a grim smile on his mouth. "You and the master are two of a kind Miss Nita," he said, and admiration made his voice clear and strong. He leaned out of the window and looked for an anchor to which to toss his rope. "I'll get you out of this, or die!"

Nita stood just beside him, and there was a fierce exultation rising within her. "We must both live, Jackson," she said slowly. "We must carry on the work of the Spider… and we must avenge him!"

Her face was uplifted, her eyes bent on the cold glitter of the stars above and there was a steady, proud smile on her lips. She did not hear the pounding of the police, smashing at the door, nor their shouts.

"Ready, Miss Nita," Jackson whispered.

Nita said, "Yes." There was a wet tracery of tears across her cheek. The Black Widow....

CHAPTER 6
RETURN FROM THE DEAD

BEFORE HIS eyes opened—before even his will had begun to fight its way upward from the black depths—Richard Wentworth realized his whereabouts. The antiseptic smell, the crawling pain in body and brain had marked too many awakenings for him to fail to identify a hospital bed. For just that moment, while realization swam into his consciousness, Wentworth kept his eyes closed. There had been that bullet in his side. Slowly, he expanded his lungs, waiting for the twinge of pain—and none came. The surprise of it flung his eyes wide and his hand moved hesitantly to the wound, and found not even a bandage.

A man's flushed face was bent over him, a young face beneath a mop of curly black hair. The eyes were magnified by the lens of spectacles and excitement was in them.

"Know me?" the man asked eagerly.

Probing his side with his fingers, finding only the slight soreness of an almost healed wound, Wentworth racked his brain for an answer... and found that in the young doctor's face. Wentworth smiled faintly.

"I suppose I should," he said slowly. "There must have been a head injury, too. How long have I been here?"

The young doctor straightened and the flush in his cheeks deepened. His laughter held triumph. "You see, sir," he said, "a complete release from trauma. The amnesia has dissipated."

Wentworth turned his head slightly and saw the serious mien of another, older man who obviously was also a physician.

The man nodded gravely. "You are to be congratulated, Morgan," he said.

The young doctor, Morgan, was bubbling with words and from them Wentworth gathered a summary of the lapse of time. Picked up in a roadside ditch, a charity patient, he had suffered a complete amnesia from a skull fracture that had required trephining. Morgan had performed a second operation to dissipate a blood clot that was pressing on the brain, an operation to which other doctors had objected… Morgan was enjoying his triumph now. Wentworth saw that, except as a case, he was unimportant to the doctors. He had been mistaken for a homeless vagrant….

"You'll be right as rain in six months," Morgan smiled benevolently down upon Wentworth. "I had to put a silver plate in your skull. You'll have headaches for a while, of course, and you'll have to be careful of exertion or violent excitement for some time to come. Vertigo, you know. Perhaps, even a return of the amnesia, but I'm sure there will be no permanent ill effects. Six months rest… You can tell us now who you are, can't you? I'll need the data for a paper I'm preparing…."

Wentworth closed his eyes. "I remember," he said, faintly.

"Charles McQuade. No home. No relatives. I happened to see a bank robbery in Albany and the crooks kidnaped and shot me. I remember being shot, but I still can't recall what the men looked like or anything like that. Maybe later it will come back to me."

"I'm sure it will," Morgan said eagerly. "You must rest now. That's the secret. Rest. Complete rest."

Wentworth made no answer. Morgan was right about one thing, at any rate. He had the headache… His brain was whirling with the implications of a month's amnesia. A *month*… Dear God, what had happened in New York during those fleet, blank days? What had *"he"* done? How many scores had been murdered? And Nita would believe him dead….

It took a violent effort of will to choke off his thoughts and force himself back into the depths of sleep. A silver plate in his skull and a warning that exertion or excitement would bring unconsciousness and perhaps amnesia. Six months… Wentworth fought down an urge to wild laughter. It would be a feeble and crippled Spider who returned to battle the horror of this new Underworld butcher, but he would return—and soon!

That same night, Wentworth began his campaign of return, began it by weakly dragging himself from bed—an effort that almost plunged him fainting to the floor. He surveyed his enfeebled limbs, examined the healing wound in his side. Standing grimly there beside his bed, a gaunt skeleton of a man, with a bandaged head, Wentworth made his calculations. This was a road he knew well, and he knew, better than these doctors, the precise recuperative powers of his body. He must lose another two weeks before he could hope to attempt a return. Two weeks, sleep and forced eating and, at night, a gradual course of exercises....

IT WAS one night over two weeks later, and well along toward dawn, when Wentworth finally discharged himself from treatment. He had gauged his time carefully, from frequent observations. He knew at just which time the night nurse chose to snatch a brief nap. During this period, he slipped silently along the corridors to the internes' quarters where he confiscated clothing, a few dollars. He made certain of the man's name, from a label on the door, and determined to pay him back a hundredfold at the first opportunity. These poor devils made little enough....

Once dressed, it was not difficult to walk from the hospital and take to the highway. His plans were carefully laid and adroit questioning had netted him the direction and distance of a nearby minor airport.

The two-mile walk almost exhausted his small vitality and he was forced to rest a long while before he could undertake the next step of his program. He played in luck then for, just at dawn, a small sport cabin plane was wheeled from a hangar by a mechanic. The motor exploded into life and, afterward, the mechanic left it with idling engine on the tarmac in the windless dawn. Minutes later, Wentworth slipped into the closed cabin of the ship, jumped it over the chocks, and sent it skimming down the field and into the brightening sky.

He was shivering, partly from cold but more from exhaustion, yet his hand was sure upon the stick and he held the throttle cracked to the last notch. Everything depended now upon speed.

If he could reach New York before the warning was broadcast to watch out for a stolen plane, his course would be simplified. If the alarm was spread… Wentworth's lips tightened. They would not find even a weakened Spider easy to capture!

He knew that he could not any longer delay his return. The papers which he could obtain in the hospital were full of the depredations of the man the reporters had christened the Butcher. And the night before, a singer had been slaughtered at the Club Angelic and the manager, Manuel Lopez, shot down and marked with a black spider. The newspapers were pointing eagerly to the fact that Lopez had been the chief witness against Richard Wentworth, and they were speculating on the connection of the Spider and the Butcher….

Before he had been fifteen minutes in the air, the radio of the plane wakened with the news of his theft of the ship and a request that all airports watch out for him—that he had headed in the direction of New York City. It was over the northernmost limits of the Bronx that Wentworth became suddenly aware of another, swifter ship diving toward him from the sun—and heard a challenge from its pilot slam in through the radio.

"Turn eastward, plane NC-17," came the order. "Turn eastward and land at the civic airport, North Beach. This is the New York Police speaking!"

Wentworth swore and held steadily to his course. The police plane could follow him to a landing, but as long as he kept over city streets, no more than that. Trailing him in was bad enough, God knew. In his weakened condition, swift flight would be almost impossible; and capture meant identification and impris-

Wentworth slammed the
plane to earth—between
two light-posts!

onment on the charge of murdering Fritz Street. District Attorney Wilton Foley would be very remiss if he did not find a way also to charge him with the death of Manuel Lopez!

THE POLICE pilot's radio orders were becoming more peremptory and, irritably, Wentworth switched off the receiving

87

set. He scanned the earth below for a possible landing place. It could not be anything as easy as the municipal golf links at Van Courtlandt Park, for the police plane could follow him easily there.

Wentworth swore softly. Only one thing could avail. He must make a crash landing in a city street and trust to his superlative ability as a pilot to come through safely. The radio pilot would not dare follow him; and if he made the set-down swiftly enough, there would not be time for the pilot to summon radio patrol cars.

Once the decision was made, Wentworth acted upon it swiftly. The hour was early still, the streets mostly deserted. He would pick a spot near a subway entrance... Deliberately, his lips bloodless with compression, Wentworth tightened the safety belt about his waist. He could not risk being thrown. The slightest blow on his head would be fatal to his plans. Angrily, he fought the unaccustomed trembling of his hands.

He had far over-reached his strength. Well, once down, he could rest. He still had a car hidden away in a garage on the west side. Weapons were there, a small store of money, change of clothing. He concentrated on this while he made his swift selection of a narrow street that slanted steeply uphill toward a subway station. He needed this reassurance of rest to stimulate his failing endurance.

Once the street was selected, Wentworth threw the plane into a swift dive. An ironic smile twisted his lips as he saw the police ship sweep toward him... too late. The pilot had not anticipated such a move and could not head him off. The wind whined through the struts and the pitch mounted steadily. The narrow canyon between low tenement and apartment buildings rushed to meet him. A man in his shirt sleeves stood yawning on the doorstep, heard the shriek of the diving plane and stiffened ludicrously, arms still stretched high above his head. He turned and darted into the shelter of the doorway.

Wentworth was a scant hundred feet above the rooftops and the tricky cross-currents of canyon-distorted winds struck and buffeted the plane. He was swept wide of the street, a roof swooped up to meet him. A kick on the rudder, a sharp bank and he was whipping into the street itself. He was below the level of the roof-tops, fighting to keep his wings away from the walls.

White faces at the windows screamed with wide open mouths. At the corner, a man in police blue darted out suddenly, stood stiffly for a second, then ripped out a revolver and fired blindly in the general direction of the plane—trying to warn Wentworth off.

Wentworth swore. Didn't the fool realize that if a bullet should find him, it would mean a smash into the walls… and death for any unfortunate who happened to be in the rooms beyond them? A downdraft sucked the ship toward the pavement, and Wentworth yanked the throttle wide for an instant before he slammed it shut and cut the engine. Too late to change plans now.

With a final shot, the policeman scuttled for the protection of the corner. That last spurt of the engine had been unavoidable, but it was dooming Wentworth's plans. He would sweep past the corner and the cross-draft would make him crash.

Deliberately, Wentworth took the only chance that offered. He kicked the plane closer to earth, slammed it in between the two light-posts at the corner. He surged forward in the straps as the posts bit into the wings, sheared them off clean—but the plane's speed was out by two-thirds.

Wentworth's head was reeling from the jar, but his hands knew what to do. He slapped the tail-skid to earth, savagely. The front wheels pulled down, bounced, lunged forward. Wentworth fought fiercely with the rudder. The stubs of wings helped slightly. The ship settled again, veered in the cross-draft of the corner. The wheels bumped the curb and, with a splintering jar, the propeller rammed into the corner of a building.

For a long instant, the breath squeezed out of him by his lurch in the belts, Wentworth wavered in his seat. But his hands were already at work upon the belts. They came free and he batted open the door of the cabin, staggered to the pavement. He pitched to his knees, reeled blindly to his feet and was running. The subway kiosk was less than fifty feet away. Behind him, his motor-deafened ears caught the hoarse shouts of the policeman. A bullet whined past his ear…The damned fool was crazed with excitement; didn't know what he was doing.

Wentworth's heart was hammering in his throat, his breath was brassy in his mouth. There was no feeling in his feet and a curious lightness pulsed through his brain. Probably, it was his erratic course that saved him from the flung bullets of the pursuing policeman; perhaps the luck that had deserted him a month before had returned at last. He made the subway stairs, fell more than ran down them and caught a train an instant before it pulled out from the station.

He sagged into a seat in a car, empty except for himself and a sleeping man, and for a while blackness pumped at his brain. That faded, but fatigue had him by the throat. It took a violent exertion of will to drive himself to his feet and change to the last mode of conveyance they would expect a fugitive to use: one of the rumbling leisurely street cars that clattered their eccentric way at cross-town angles through the city.

Eventually, he took another subway train, changed ultimately to a cross-town bus that would take him within two blocks of the private garage where he stored the car. It took his last strength to walk those two blocks and he was reeling like a drunken man when he turned into the mouth of the alley on which the garage opened. He paused then, bracing a shoulder against the brick wall, breathing shallowly. Death had waited for him in that other garage. If there were enemies here then....

THE ALLEY seemed empty. He stumbled on, trying to force his senses to the preternatural sharpness that, more times than he could remember, had snatched the Spider from the brink of death. He heard a siren, faint with distance, whimper across the city blocks. A truck rumbled past the alley's end. He dragged his feet toward the garage, wavered as he stood regarding the closed doors. There was a galvanized ash can standing beside them, filled with ashes and a miscellany of bottles and cans. Ashes... and it was midsummer! Also, now that Wentworth's alert suspicions were aroused, he could see that the car was quite new and had been deliberately marred and aged. His narrowed eyes detected next a raw red place where bricks had been chipped away, or drilled—in the wall just behind the can.

And yet it was not conscious thought that analyzed these details. Some secret part of his mind was operating despite the bankruptcy of his vitality—the same subtle mental reflexes that had snatched him before this from a hundred apparently inescapable dilemmas. The sense of danger sharpened all his perceptions. Now he heard sounds that, before this, his blurred faculties had missed.

A window creaked faintly, being raised very slowly; there was the oily smooth rush of an opening door somewhere behind him and then the muted rasp of a man creeping. Trapped! There could be no other meaning for these things. The garage had been turned into a trap. Behind that can were the wires either of an alarm or a dictograph and men were creeping toward him. But these were scarcely the methods of the Butcher. Then... *the police!*

Behind his body, Wentworth's left hand flicked out and caught up a whiskey bottle from the trash can. The rustle of feet was closer and, in the long shadows thrown by the early rays of the sun, he read the confirmation of his fears. The men behind him were two in number, they wore the uniform caps of the police—and there were guns ready in their fists!

Equally impossible for Wentworth to fight, or to run in his weakened condition. Yet capture would doom his plans for fighting the Butcher, doom the Spider as well! Wentworth gripped the bottle, but only as a weapon for his wits. With the two police less than ten feet behind him, he lifted the bottle before his eyes and, peering at it, swayed uncertainly on his feet. He cursed then in a thickened voice, hurled the bottle away from him to shatter against the wall. He took a faltering step forward, a drunken derelict in disreputable clothing, without a hat. There had been nothing in his behavior since entering the alley to contradict that fact and, for the first time, he was glad for the weakness that harassed him. It would help out now.

Wentworth saw, by the shadows on the ground, that the two policemen had halted. He took another faltering step, then stopped with his legs spraddled wide and bent far forward. He made his stomach retch, staggered until he leaned against the wall. The hand that apparently pressed hard against his face actually thrust a finger down his throat and nausea shook him. The violence of it almost completed the disintegration of his strength. He leaned weakly against the wall and his body shook.

Finally, he thrust free of the wall and began a stumbling, hesitant course along the alley, reeled around until he was facing the police. The two uniformed men were staring at him, nonplussed, guns hanging at their sides. Wentworth swayed on his feet and surveyed them owlishly. Then he waved a limp hand in salute.

"How ya, pal?" he mumbled. "S'lousy booze you get these days, hunh? Ought to be 'gainst the law. Why'n hell don't you do something about it? Cops, aren't you? Lousy liquor."

He reeled past them, mumbling to himself. The two cops grinned, shrugged and holstered their guns. From above, a man's voice suddenly called out sharply, *"Search him!"*

And Wentworth had no gun, had nothing save a few crumpled dollar bills. He protested indignantly, was allowed to stumble on, followed by the good-natured jibes of the police.

It was just as he reached the mouth of the alley that he saw the coupé rolling toward him and recognized it incredulously as a duplicate of the car he had supposed was stored in the garage. The license plates... It was his car! And then he realized that the girl behind the wheel was... *Nita van Sloan!*

HE SAW recognition gladden her face, saw the coupé jerk to a halt... and knew suddenly how the whole trap had been set. The police had followed Nita to this spot—the police who still were watching his stumbling progress.

If Nita ran up to him—and she was already opening the door of the car—they would become suspicious again. If they examined him closely—if they took his fingerprints—he was doomed! Fantastic that his heart should leap with gladness at the sight of Nita—and that he must deny her or land them both behind the bars. Pain in his breast, and his brain so weary....

Almost, he despaired; almost, he reeled toward Nita to clasp her in his arms, be it for ever so brief a moment. He had been a madman to drag his enfeebled body back so soon to the battle. He was outclassed, beaten. So his heart, and perhaps his desire dictated... but that cold, calm brain of his clicked on.

Nita was climbing from the car, but she was out of sight of the police. Wentworth reeled about so that he faced back into the alley and began to mumble curses again.

"I'm a taxpayer," he cried hoarsely. "You cops can't do things like this to me. Let them sell lousy liquor and then maul a man around. You can't do this to me. I'll see the district leader, that's what I'll do. Lousy cops mauling a taxpayer."

He could not look toward Nita, dared not. If she showed herself in the mouth of the alley, she would be recognized. It must be that way, since police had followed her here. Only his extreme emaciation, and the drunken stupidity he had put upon his face, had prevented his own identification. He took a stumbling step toward the policemen. They were still grinning and one of them swung his hand.

"That's right," he called. "You run along and see your district leader."

Wentworth sucked in a slow breath of exquisite relief. Even if Nita had failed to get the significance of his own words, that call would warn her. He stood swaying there for a moment longer, shouting things at the two cops. Then he veered suddenly about and staggered back to the mouth of the alley. Nita was climbing into the coupé, her face frightened and pale. There was suffering there, too, and her eyes pleaded with him. She, too, felt the misery of this moment, separated for so long from the man she loved, whom she must of necessity believe dead and then, in this instant of meeting, each must deny the other—lest the comfort for which both longed bring them to their doom!

He reeled around the corner away from Nita's coupé, heading in the opposite direction. With that gesture, he indicated more plainly than any words that she was not to follow him. He staggered, and there was nothing deliberated in his loss of balance. He leaned against the wall through a long moment, gathering strength, before he could move on.

He heard the coupé start forward and, even through the blur of the engine, he thought he could hear Nita catch a sob in her throat. Nita… For her own sake, he must run from her. Somehow, he must evade her surveillance. Regardless of danger to themselves, she would not desert him in his weakness. He cursed the exhaustion which had made him stagger. He fought on along the empty street, methodically setting down each foot. It was painfully slow… and he had no haven now; no refuge. Beaten….

CHAPTER 7
DEAD MAN'S BATTLE

A S SOON as Nita's coupé rounded the corner out of sight, Wentworth angled across the street to the continuation of the alley and pushed on as rapidly as possible. Nita was sure to circle and attempt to help him. This was the only means he could figure, in his weakened condition, by which he might elude her. He did not again sight the coupé, and presently he stumbled into a diner and ordered food.

He sat there a long time, trying to chart a course of action against the Butcher. He was renewing the battle under terrific handicaps, and he realized he was without any information which might point either to the man's identity or to his headquarters since the destruction of the Van Schlaick home.

Abruptly, he became aware that the radio was blaring out the news of his airplane crash in the upper city, shifting from that to the latest catastrophic assault of the Butcher. Last night, explosion had destroyed a "dance palace" and from the debris eighty-five bodies had been taken....

"There seems to be utterly no purpose behind these massacres," the announcer declared, "other than a wanton desire to kill and kill and kill. The police are no nearer capturing the Butcher, though they pretend to hold the man known as the Spider responsible for these crimes...."

The words goaded Wentworth out of the lethargy into which he had fallen and he realized that while he had sat here, only vaguely conscious of his surroundings, hours had slipped past. He had reached no resolution about future action against the Butcher, but this fresh news made it abundantly clear that he must strike quickly. The police were at a loss and daily, the Butcher added fresh scores to the already staggering total of his victims.

It came to Wentworth that some criminal underlings of the Butcher undoubtedly had been accustomed to frequent the saloon from which he had first made contact with the Hounds of Hell. That was his only definite point of contact, and it was the one he must use... not, of course, as Blinky McQuade since it was in that guise he first had met Van Schlaick. For the same reason, he could not risk a return to Blinky's quarters which ordinarily would offer a refuge....

Wentworth lurched to his feet and pushed resolutely to the street. Food and rest had strengthened him but there was a dragging slowness to all his movements. Throughout the day, he would rest and gather his forces—a sunny bench in the park would serve excellently—and tonight he would visit the saloon and endeavor to enlist in the Butcher's murder mob! It was a daring and dangerous course but none other was open to him and he would not shirk his duty. The Spider had set his foot in the trail and, from that pursuit, only death could turn him aside....

It was as a walking travesty of death that Wentworth invaded the saloon that night. From his small store of stolen money he had purchased certain adjuncts to make-up. The pallor of his face was death-like and the shadows beneath his eyes took on a brownish cast; the gouged-out lines of suffering about his mouth were sharpened to bitterness.

He was as different as possible from Blinky McQuade and he walked with a belligerent swagger to the bar and ordered a drink in a rasping, bullying voice. It was clever work. Criminals would look askance at a cringing man and suspect such a stranger of playing the spy. It would not occur to them that a deliberately conspicuous unknown would have anything to hide—or so Wentworth hoped!

He tossed off his drink and the liquor lighted a fire in his stomach, spread a false glow through his veins. Tonight, he felt old and worn and the memory of Nita's glad face in that first instant of beholding him was a mockery. It put a bitterness in his mouth, recklessness in his blood. He looked about him with boldly challenging eyes and few met his stare directly. There were men here who had on that other night heard the baying of the Hounds of Hell, but which of them might be the Butcher's men? A HOT glow mounted behind Wentworth's blue-gray eyes. It was a time for strong measures since each added day this new terror of the Underworld survived brought more human beings to their graves. True, Wentworth might sulk and listen, hoping to learn some plan of the Butcher's... At the thought, whispered words at his elbow caught his attention.

"Now if I was *him*," the man mumbled. "What I'd do would be knock over Madison Square Garden tonight. The big fight is on and the gate will take in plenty."

Wentworth shook his head. Idle talk, of course, that meant nothing, yet the thought nagged at the back of his mind, as he reckoned the horror of such an attack. Ten, fifteen thousand persons under a single roof; perhaps more... under a heavy roof that the mines or the explosive bullets of the Butcher might tumble crushingly upon their head! Well, if he were to prevent such massacres, he must set to work. His move was to sell these men here—some of whom certainly represented the Butcher— on the idea that he was an expert crook. What better way could he choose than... to hold up the saloon!

Wentworth discredited the idea with a smile that, on his gaunt face, harshened the bitter curve of his lips—and yet the thought persisted. It would make him a reputation in a trice. If one of the Butcher's men did not approach him afterward, at least he would be established as one of them. And, tonight, the play suited his mood. He could break it off in the middle and call it a jest....

Wentworth turned to the bar, ordered another drink and realized that he was going to do it. He knew the peril of the thing and it intoxicated him. A fragmentary memory of the warning the young doctor of the hospital had uttered crossed his mind;

high excitement might produce vertigo. Ridiculous. What was there in such a proceeding to excite… the Spider! He would need a gun, first.

Practiced eyes soon spotted the men who carried guns, and it included most of those in the room. He waited until one, more drunken than the rest, staggered toward the washroom and, presently, Wentworth followed. He strode long-legged, gaunt as a crane, and eyes followed him with furtive speculation.

In the washroom, he acted without hesitation. He jabbed stiffened fingers into the side of the criminal's neck and let him fall to the floor because he had not the strength to ease the man down. The gun was a stubby .38 and there were extra cartridges. Without compunction, Wentworth helped himself to money from the man's wallet. His lips twitched a little. This was scarcely worthy game for the Spider, but he would need money, and saloon gunmen scarcely came by theirs honestly.

Wentworth weighed the revolver in his hand, nodded over the comfortable feel of it, then tucked the gun into the waistband of his trousers just hidden by the hang of his coat. His plan was already made. He strode out of the washroom.

There was one man standing at the end of the bar near the cash-register and the bartender was close by, polishing a glass. Two long steps took Wentworth to the spot. His left fist drove accurately in beneath the customer's ear and the gun flipped into his right hand, covered the bartender, swept purposefully across the others at their tables, at the bar.

"Don't disturb yourselves, gentlemen," Wentworth said casually. "My business is with your host. This is a stick-up."

There was no movement at all for a long moment in that smoke-dimmed long barroom. Outside in the street, an automobile spurted past the door and children were screaming in a nameless game. The men along the bar were frozen in stiff attitudes; there were drinks half-raised and one man strangled on a mouthful of liquor, fought wildly to stay the convulsive jerking of his head and body. It was the only sound. These men recognized the practiced firmness of that leveled revolver, and the authority of that casual voice.

"Fine," Wentworth nodded. "Mine host, I'll relieve you only of the bills in the large denomination slot. Open the drawer and pass them over. Carefully. Carefully."

The bar-keep's face was a sullen red and his hands trembled as he stiffly punched a button to open the cash-register and fumbled with the bills. He tossed them to the counter, keeping carefully away from Wentworth's leveled gun. Wentworth laughed and brushed them back.

"Keep them, bar-keep," Wentworth said. "Set up drinks for the boys. Things are just a bit too quiet to suit me. When Death Hawkins comes to town, *things happen!*"

The bartender was staring at him stupidly, and a ripple ran along the men at the bar. Wentworth let his gun rest on the mahogany, but kept it in his hand.

"Come, come, don't you gentlemen appreciate my humor?" he asked. "In Chicago, they have a heartier brand of laughter. *It's* a joke, fools. Bar-keep, take back your money. I don't need it. Death Hawkins doesn't bother with chicken feed."

One of the men along the bar burst out in a sudden guffaw.

"By God, he did it for a joke. He stuck up Toughy O'Brien for a joke, and with us here. My God!"

WENTWORTH THRUST the revolver back into his waistband, but handy to his draw, and he saw a sudden shift in the eyes of the men. They were no longer looking into his face; they were looking behind him! With an oath, he started to whirl. He ducked his head and started a spin to his left and something struck with dull agony across the back of his skull. He didn't know that he could still feel so much pain. The room wheeled. The gun was in his hand, but he hadn't fired when he heard the crashing roar of a shot.

He could just glimpse his assailant out of the corner of his eye—the man he had slugged in the washroom. His blow had been weak, then. But the man was no longer attacking. He was sagging backward, his head wrenched at an unnatural angle back between his shoulders—and there was a blue hole between his eyes! So much Wentworth saw in that brief moment when his brain was being ripped asunder by pain.

There was frantic movement all around him, the tramp of feet and curses. Wentworth speared a hand to the bar and hung on grimly, fighting the rubber from his knees while the roaring went on in his head. He heard a voice, a woman's voice.

"Stand still, fools," it ordered curtly. "There are more bullets in this gun and they can travel straight. This way... This way, Death Hawkins."

Wentworth tried to shake the daze from his brain. Surely, that was Nita speaking to him, Nita calling to him from the door of the saloon. His hand was white with gripping the bar and, slowly, the room swam back into focus. Men had leaped back from the bar and there was a fierce rage on the faces of some; rage, but fear also. And in the doorway… God, it *was* Nita! He knew her despite the black mask that covered her entire face save where her eyes peered through slits. The twin guns in her hands were very steady.

She said again, "This way, Death Hawkins." An urgency had crept into her voice and Wentworth heard silence, an aching silence in the street. No children laughing and screaming there now. The alarm had been given. In a few moments, the police would be here, and there was a dead man on the floor whom Nita had slain to save him.

Wentworth forced stiffness into his knees, loosened his grip on the counter to scoop up the money that still lay there. He moved along the emptied bar with his head up, and the gun careless in his fingers.

"It seems," he said clearly, "that you don't appreciate the humor of Death Hawkins. Remember to laugh next time you see me. And laugh hard… *or you may not laugh again!*"

He was backing up beside Nita and laughter pumped out of his own throat. It was queer strained stuff to hear, a little mad perhaps. Then they were backing together toward the door. There was a reeling lightness in his head and it widened his eyes with menace. The gun in his right hand was nervous as a coiled snake, and as deadly. In all that barroom, not a man moved or seemed to breathe. Wentworth fumbled behind him for the bat-wing doors, pushed them wide.

"Go ahead," Nita said calmly. "The car's by the door, to the right."

Wentworth obeyed. There was no speed in his legs and the world was swimming about him again. He turned and took awkward strides, fumbled into the right hand seat of the coupé parked there.

Nita was running toward him and he twisted about and sent a bullet slamming in through the batwing doors, then another… another. Nita was behind the wheel, and the car leaped forward. It was taking the corner on screaming tires before the first man showed himself at the door of the saloon, but he was running, at high speed… and he went in the opposite direction. Those men with illegal guns would want to get away before the police came and found a murdered man and a looted till.

So much Wentworth saw and then his powerful will relaxed and the darkness clustered about his brain.

HE DID not quite lose consciousness. He knew that the coupé slammed through the streets and presently moved more slowly. He heard a shrieking of sirens that faded out behind. Nita was glancing toward him anxiously now and he tried to reassure her with words, but they mumbled unintelligibly on his lips.

"It's all right now, Dick," Nita said softly. "It's all right. But promise me you won't ever try to run away from me again."

The coolness of the night wind eased the pressure about his temples and he could presently look toward Nita and smile faintly. "Death Hawkins didn't do so well in his first appearance in New York," he murmured. "And don't feel badly about the man you shot. He was Fritz Street's chief executioner."

"I wouldn't in any case," Nita's voice was low, but it held an implacable note. "I read of the treatment given you in the hospital up-state, though of course they don't know your name. He… He was *hitting* your poor head!"

"Lopez?" Wentworth questioned softly.

Nita told him about it then. "There is something being planned tonight," she said, and there was a worried crease between her brows. "I don't know just what, but the Butcher is certainly going to strike some new blow. This girl who saw me in Lopez's office, I feared. I could see no mention of her in the newspapers and tonight I found her."

"You wore your mask!" Wentworth asked sharply.

Nita nodded. "I saw no need to give her another look at my face," she said. "But it seems I need not have bothered. She didn't know who I was and didn't care. She attacked me in Lopez's office because if she had not done so, and I had failed as she expected, Lopez would have… taken care of her afterward. The phrase is her own and the way she said it was… *frightful.* She was taken away by two men who warned her that she would be called on presently to testify to what she had seen. If she tried to run away, *"he"* would find her with the Hounds of Hell… And tonight she was telephoned and warned not to leave the house as she had planned."

Wentworth swore softly, pushing himself erect on the cushions. He was aware of dark streets drifting past slowly as Nita sent the coupé leisurely through back lanes of the city. The lights had a strange soft warmth, as always when summer was upon the city, but there was curiously little loitering on the streets.

Windows were mostly covered by drawn shades. Wentworth knew that they rode through a city subdued by terror, by the dread of explosions which might blast the roof down over your head, or might merely tear your body to bits. And tonight, the Butcher would strike again....

"Where is this girl?" Wentworth asked, his voice hoarse. "We must get to her right away."

Nita stared at him with widened eyes. "I took her to a hotel and registered her under another name. She was... grateful. Finding her at first was simple enough. I looked over publicity pictures of the girls who performed at the Club Angelic until I identified her, then found her address. I don't understand."

Wentworth's face held a keen, strained look. His words came out choppily. "Simple enough. The Butcher knows that you killed Lopez and why. The girl can identify you. He's saving her until the time is ripe for her testimony."

"But what can she tell?"

"She knows," Wentworth said softly, "where the Butcher will strike tonight! Quickly, Nita, find a telephone!"

The coupé leaped forward under Nita's hands, but still she shook her head. "I don't understand," she insisted. "If she had known, I think she would have told me."

"She had a date to go out," Wentworth said. "The Butcher wants her alive."

Nita gasped, swung the coupé westward and headed for better lighted streets. "You mean that the place the Butcher is going to destroy is the same one to which she was going tonight? Oh, you must be right. I hope... I hope we're in time!"

"We have to be," Wentworth sat tensely forward, a hand braced against the dashboard. "You must call her. She should recognize your voice. Ask her simply where she was going tonight."

WENTWORTH'S MIND was clicking with a calm, cold certainty. He thought that the police would, this time, heed a warning that came from the Spider. His own purposes were different than the work of clearing whatever place was menaced by the Butcher. He knew by now that *"he"* did not attend in person the scenes of his massacres. His underlings would be there, and it was Wentworth's chance to form the contact that he had attempted there in the saloon when his plans had miscarried so woefully. He would join the Butcher's mob, either in his own assumed identity, or in that of one of *his* men.

"I must find out who the Butcher is," he said slowly. "I have no strength for pitched battle. When I find him…."

Nita glanced at him and there was a painful doubt in her eyes. "Dick," she said, "you may not like what you find."

There was something in the tone of her voice that pulled Wentworth's head sharply toward her. "What do you mean?"

Nita hesitated and he saw her white teeth pinch the fullness of her lower lip. He leaned toward her. "Why should you hesitate, dear?" he asked quietly. "If it is because I am weakened…."

Nita shook her head. "It is not that. I didn't tell you everything that happened in the office of Manuel Lopez. He was talking over the telephone to someone he called Kirkpatrick…."

"Kirkpatrick!" The name exploded from Wentworth's lips.

THE SPIDER

"But that's errant nonsense. Or at least, it couldn't be old Kirk. Aside from everything else, he's on the other side of the world!"

"The first three numbers Lopez dialed," Nita said slowly, "were the first three of Kirkpatrick's private home phone. The unlisted one."

Wentworth drew in a slow heavy breath. "It must be investigated, of course," he said dully.

Nita said, "Yes. I have taken an apartment in the same building with Stanley's. And I sent a radiogram to Doctor Smithers, who went with him on the voyage."

"The answer?" Wentworth's voice was strangely shaken. No two men had ever been closer than he and Kirkpatrick, for all that the police commissioner had hounded the Spider through the years of his activity. But Kirk was a man of unswerving integrity. They were as close as brothers. Yet, when Wentworth had been in the death-house once on a frame-up that had almost cost his life, Kirkpatrick, then governor of the state and convinced of his guilt, had refused even a reprieve....

"Damn it," he said violently. "It simply isn't possible."

Nita said, "I feel that way, but I had to try. There has been no answer yet to my radio."

Wentworth leaned back in a corner of the cushions and closed his eyes. He was remembering that there had been a death-trap for him in his other garage; and that outside of his intimate circle only Kirkpatrick had *known* of that garage.

"I wouldn't believe it," he said slowly, "if Kirk confessed it to me with his own lips."

Nita made no answer, but there was worry in her eyes as she

jerked the coupé to the curb. "You want me to phone, Dick?" she asked. "This isn't just a trick so that you can escape from me? You need me now, Dick, and I… I need you."

Wentworth smiled and pressed her slim hand. "I'll be here, dear, when you return."

Nita left without another word and Wentworth, waiting grimly in the darkness, laid his own rapid plans. His plight and the future of the city could not possibly be darker. Both Nita and he were without any clue to the Butcher, and he could not believe that the police were in any better state. The fiend struck when and where he would and the death toll of his crimes already had passed the thousand mark. Nita had hit on the solution of these crimes in that she knew the motive. What made it the more damnable was that, if men were frightened into paying extortion, they'd be too terrified to testify against the Butcher.

Those whom the Butcher struck would never live to tell what they knew. In many cases Wentworth was convinced they did not even have warning, but were destroyed as an example to others on whom pressure was being applied. So there was nothing to point to the identity of the men who were being blackmailed by terror. An air-tight scheme and the very wantonness with which the Butcher killed produced its own immunity. Kirkpatrick involved in such a horror? It was incredible, completely beyond belief.

Wentworth realized that the necessity of repeating that fact in his own mind meant that doubts had arisen. Kirkpatrick, as he knew him, could not be capable of these things, but suppose… suppose his illness had warped his great brain? Wentworth thrust the thought from him, returned to his own immediate problem. He must send Nita to safety, and then....

NITA WAS running as she burst out of the drugstore and flung herself behind the wheel. "She has left the hotel," Nita said rapidly, "but the clerk told me that, before she went out, she had them obtain for her... two tickets to the championship fight at Madison Square Garden. The tickets had been previously held in reserve in her name."

Wentworth felt an uncontrollable shudder trace its cold way over his body. Ten, fifteen thousand people in the Garden, and the monstrous madman whose other name was Murder could bring the whole, massive roof down upon their heads! He spoke in a strained voice.

"I'm going to call the police," he said, "and try to make them believe. I would be helpless, alone, to clear the Garden. Then I'll go on and... do what I can. You, Nita, must go and keep a constant watch over Kirkpatrick's apartment. There is a meaning behind these things, but I cannot believe that Kirkpatrick himself is involved."

Nita glanced swiftly at his resolute profile. "You are trying to remove me from danger. I won't go!"

Wentworth shook his head rigidly. "I am sending you into danger. The crux of this whole case is in the strange use of Kirkpatrick's name."

Nita hesitated and her hands were white with the pressure of her grip upon the wheel. "I will go on one condition, Dick," she said slowly. "That you promise me, at the first possible moment, to join me there. At my apartment."

Wentworth nodded, a smile twisting his lips wryly. What he promised, he would always perform… if he lived.

"I promise you, dear," he said. "Now stop the car where you can get a cab and I can reach a phone."

Nita's face softened, and yet there was anxiety behind her eyes. She found the spot and parked the car, put her arms gently about Wentworth's neck and drew his cheek to hers. For an instant, she held him so, then she straightened and stepped to the pavement. "I consent to go, Dick, because I know, even more than you, how important it is that a watch be kept on Kirkpatrick's apartment. While I was in the store telephoning, I put through a call to the radio people."

"There was an answer!" Wentworth's voice lifted sharply.

"There was an answer," Nita agreed. "Doctor Smithers radioed me… He radioed me that Kirkpatrick disappeared from the liner three weeks ago in Shanghai! He said that since the very beginning of the voyage, Stanley had been behaving queerly. Doctor Smithers said… He said that he thought Stanley Kirkpatrick had gone insane!" She paled.

CHAPTER 8
DEATH'S SPECIAL RECRUIT

THE URGENCY of the crisis gave Wentworth a false strength and, after phoning a warning to the police, he hurled the coupé northward toward Madison Square Garden. What course he would follow when he reached the huge sports arena, he could not determine in advance. He had made no secret of his identity in calling the police, but had frankly announced himself as the Spider. Time was when that would have been sufficient and the entire organization of the police would have been thrown into the battle. But now he could not even guess at the result. The Butcher had played his cards well indeed in alienating both Wentworth and the Spider from the police!

It was Wentworth's guess that the police would attempt an investigation. They could not afford to ignore the warning, for Wentworth had told them the same information was being sent to the newspapers. If, after that, his admonition proved accurate, the police would be hard put to explain their failure. However, only a prompt emptying of the Garden could, by any stretch of imagination, possibly avail to prevent the wholesale slaughter that had been planned. And the police would not be likely to take so drastic an action without the inevitable "investigation."

These thoughts brought home to Wentworth the utter futility so far of all his efforts even to thwart the occasional mass attacks of the Butcher. At whatever cost to himself, he must make contact and press home his attack… tonight!

For a moment, Wentworth's thoughts lingered with Nita and the incredible things she had discovered about Stanley Kirkpatrick. The radiogram from Dr. Smithers seemed terribly to confirm the suspicions that arose against his will concerning his friend. But he had not exaggerated to Nita his belief in Kirkpatrick. *"Even if he confessed to me with his own lips…"* Yes, but there, too, there must be an accounting without delay. Wentworth's mouth was a lipless gash, pain and despair in his soul. His body was so weak and the odds against him were so great. With him, he knew, the fate of a city rode this night!

Wentworth had sliced over to Eighth Avenue and, far ahead near Madison Square Garden, he heard the brief moan of sirens. The first of the radio cars had arrived ahead of him, but he could not hope that their orders included the clearing of the Garden. He bent more tautly over the wheel, bore down on the accelerator. The soft warmth of the summer night was a mockery. There in that vast arena, thousands of fight fans were roaring in vicarious wrath over the heavyweight contenders—and soon that roar might change to another, more devastating sound. The Butcher's powerful explosives could make a wreck of that steel-groined ceiling, bring it down upon their heads, tumble the walls in upon the helpless people!

Only five blocks away… and the crash might come at any moment. The box office would be counting up receipts, and as soon as that was finished, the money would be carted off to a night depository. The crooks would strike before that. Regardless of their motive for destroying the sports palace, they would grab that money—and the blasting of the Garden would follow to cover their tracks!

Unless the police were already at work, Wentworth determined to smash his way into the Garden. If he could reach the loud-speaker arrangement which broadcast the referee's announcements, he could start a general exodus in a space of seconds… if the police allowed him to survive that long. Two blocks further now….

A CURSE leaped to Wentworth's lips as he saw a car career

out of the street beside the Garden and race toward him. He heard the yelp as a siren got under way and, an instant later, squads of police swirled into Eighth Avenue, dropped from every kind of commandeered machine. They went into the Garden at the double-quick.

Wentworth sucked in a slow breath of relief. Plainly, that fleeing car contained the robbers and it was the confirmation that the police had needed for action. God alone knew whether they would clear the building in time. Everything in Wentworth urged that he dash after the police and try to insure that the Garden was emptied before the blow fell. He was forced to acknowledge, however, that he could be of greater service in another way—by tracking down the Butcher himself!

Within thirty feet of Wentworth the carload of fleeing bandits sped past, going in the opposite direction and, a block behind, a radio car was blaring on the trail. For an instant longer, Wentworth hesitated. Then, as the police car also whipped past, he spun his own coupé in a tight U-turn and joined the chase! He had no definite plan, but the weight of his revolver pressed hard against his stomach muscles, and if he could take one of the Butcher's men prisoner, elude the police....

Straight down Eighth Avenue roared the pursuit. The police siren helped to clear the way for the fugitive car and the crimson flash of guns streaked from both machines.

Wentworth's own car, despite its shabby exterior, was far more powerful than either of the others. And, gradually, while every taut nerve in his body waited for the horror of the Garden blast, which he knew could not be much longer delayed, he narrowed the gap separating him from the police car. He had his revolver under his hand now and carefully cranked up the lower half of his windshield. The pressure of air came in like a bar of steel against his chest and face, smothering his breath in his nostrils... Then blocks had been covered and still there had been no explosion. Almost, Wentworth began to hope that he had been mistaken. Almost he dared believe that this one time the Butcher found no profit in wholesale slaughter....

Ahead of the fugitives, a traffic cop sprang out from the crowd. Warned by the sirens, he ripped out his revolver and braced it across his forearm for a precise shot at the bandits. A cry rose to Wentworth's lips, but he could not, himself, fire because the police car interposed. He swerved to the left, frantically... too late. An angry burst of flame exploded against the night where the traffic officer stood. Before the mad chase flashed by, Wentworth glimpsed a jagged hole in the pavement, and a few tattered rags of blue. That was all that remained of the daring traffic officer!

Pennsylvania Station loomed ahead, swept to the rear and still the pursuit roared on. Curses poured in a thin, whispering stream from Wentworth's lips. He wanted to take one of those crooks, at least, alive, but he could not witness this slaughter of the explosive bullets and take no action... His car heeled wildly and it took all Wentworth's strength to wrench it into a straight line. He knew without peering behind him that there was another of those jagged holes blown in the pavement where a bullet had just missed! It was five blocks afterward that Wentworth got the chance for which he had been waiting.

The bandit car swerved on shrieking tires and spurted eastward for a side street. Wentworth's gun, ready at the opening in the windshield, spoke once. Immediately, he slammed on brakes. His superlative marksmanship needed no other chance, and no confirmation. While the police driver ahead fought his bucking car into a turn, the chase ended. Wentworth's bullet found the left rear tire of the fugitive machine. It ripped entirely off with the force of the blow-out and, an instant later, the other rear tire blew, too!

The fleeing sedan flung itself into a fit of wild acrobatics. It slewed around in a complete half-circle, hit the curb broadside and somersaulted through the air toward the apartment building on the corner. It struck this upside down, rebounded and, somehow, landed on its wheels. It trundled straight across the street and found a fire-plug with its front axle. The plug tore loose and a gust of high-pressure water geysered up beneath the machine. The car stayed in that position, jiggling from the violence of the roll and the battering of the stream of water.

It seemed impossible that any occupant of the car could survive the violence of that smash-up. Yet, as the police car spun about, and one of the officers leaped out to charge down on the wreck, a gun lanced its scarlet snake-tongue from the side of the sedan. The police coupé dissolved… It jarred sideways and there was no windshield and only fragments of the top left; of the driver and the steering wheel nothing at all remained. Jockeying his car into a turn, Wentworth whipped his revolver into line on the sedan. Desperate as was the need to capture this man alive, he could not permit this wanton slaughter of the police. He could not....

He was squeezing the trigger when the deathly flame streaked out once more from the wreck and again, his coupé jarred to the concussion of those mighty bullets. The sole remaining cop... *vanished!*

Wentworth flicked on the full power of his headlights and jerked on his brakes. He flung sideways from the car, hit running and almost fell with the weakness in his legs.

"Wait!" he shouted at the blinded killer. "Wait I'm a friend!"

He ran with both hands high in the air, the gun tucked into his waistband and there was a tightness upon his lips that acknowledged the deadly peril. One more of those bullets, and... Wentworth vanished from the ken of man!

"A friend!" he called again. "I'll help you escape!"

He was still running toward the wrecked sedan when a jar caught him along the entire left side of his body. He thought for a moment, as he pitched toward the ground, that he had been hit by one of the explosive bullets. Then he heard, thinly, the tinkle of broken glass. Before it had fairly begun, that and all other sound was blotted out in a thudding roaring reverberation that seemed to jar the very bones of his body. Dazed upon the pavement, Wentworth lifted his head and stared....

NORTHWARD, WHERE the Garden stood, there was a multiple-tongued tower of scarlet flame against the night sky. It was already dying, blotted out in a roiling fountain of black smoke, in a geyser of up-cast debris. At this distance, he could see no more than that, but he knew terribly what had happened… and that the police had not arrived in time.

No more than a few minutes had elapsed in this wild pursuit. All this warning could have accomplished was to add, to the thousands of dead in that catastrophe, the squads of blue-coated police who had rushed to the rescue! Wentworth's breath was a sob on his lips as he drove himself again to his feet. His face was truly the mask of death into which he had transformed it… and he had to dissemble. He had once more to stagger toward the wrecked sedan with a cry of *"friend"* upon his lips! Only one thought sustained him. By this means, he might pierce to the heart of this murderous conspiracy; he might kill the Butcher!

He saw a man dragging himself out of the wreckage of the sedan—a man with a gun raised as alertly as the head of a coiled snake. Wentworth moved swiftly toward him, staggering from the shock of that explosion even at this distance—but with his hands resolutely lifted.

"Come on," he urged. "Come on, before the cops get here. You got the loot?"

"To hell with the loot," the man muttered thickly. "My leg is busted. Bring the car… Try any funny business and I'll blow you sky-high."

"Not a chance, pal," Wentworth said hoarsely. He darted back to his coupé, cut the headlights and rolled it swiftly up beside the man. "The cops will be busy cleaning up that mess up there for a while," he said. "Where's the loot? *'He'* ain't going to be too happy if you come back without it. *'He'* ain't going to be glad you came back alive. And maybe you won't either."

"Who in hell are you anyway?" the man muttered as Wentworth bent over him, "and what do you know…" He broke off with a groan as his broken leg sagged.

It strained Wentworth's emaciated body to the utmost to lift the man. Fortunately, he was small. He got him into the coupé by the sheer strength of his will, then staggered back toward the wreck. The inside was a shambles and the miracle was that even one man had survived.

Wentworth snatched up two satchels from the floor, paused to tuck another revolver into his waistband. It would be loaded with explosive bullets and he could not guess what emergency he must face in the immediate future. It was a wild chance he was taking. The Butcher might be grateful for the return of the loot he would believe lost, but he was too shrewd a man not to suspect Wentworth's motive.

Wentworth shot the coupé forward, but paused a half-block away to hurl an explosive bullet back into the wreck. As it disintegrated and the freed water pushed its frothing white stream into the air, Wentworth once more bore down on the accelerator.

"Where do we go from here?" he asked, but if there was laughter behind the words, it was the grim taunting laughter of the Spider that heralded his kill!

The man he had rescued was still suspicious, but was also light-headed with pain. He told Wentworth where to go and, for an instant afterward, Wentworth stared so incredulously that he almost wrecked the coupé. The headquarters of the Butcher, it appeared, were in the concrete tunnels which Wentworth himself had built beneath what was now the wreckage of his fortress home!

Now that the excitement of the chase had ended, and the full horror of the night had driven its way into his consciousness, Wentworth found himself drained of strength. His driving was faltering and uncertain. There was a question in his mind whether he could carry on with his daring plan for forcing his way into the organization of the Butcher. Perhaps he should call the police, tell them where the Butcher hid out....

Slowly, Wentworth shook his head. Even if he could be sure that the Butcher would be there—and it seemed likely that he would avoid the rendezvous of his looters until certain they had escaped surveillance—a raid by the police probably would result only in more deaths. No doubt that the place was once more mined for protection. No, he had chosen the only way. Death Hawkins, from Chicago, was taking back to the Butcher's headquarters one of the Butcher's wounded men and, what was more important, the loot of the destroyed Garden. And Death Hawkins asked in return only the privilege of joining the ranks of the master criminal's men!

It was the course the Spider had elected and in it was the only hope of destroying the Butcher himself. Wentworth knew that there was a much better chance that it would be the Spider, hunted on every hand, and feeble from recent wounds, who would himself be destroyed!

OBEYING THE instructions of the half-conscious bandit, Wentworth drove into a garage two blocks from the wreckage of his home. Three minutes later, he found himself being escorted by three armed men along a mud-walled underground passage-way which had been added to his own warrens. One of the men carried the loot; the wounded gunman was stowed away in an underground vault where a doctor already was at work on his broken leg. Wentworth reflected grimly that the Butcher took good care of his men. He had said little since driving into the garage, only demanding to be taken at once to *"him."*

His guns had been removed and the guard the men kept was sharp, businesslike. In an emergency, they would shoot and ask questions afterward, but meantime they did not talk. The very openness with which they escorted him along the corridors was ominous. It said more plainly than any threats what his fate would be. If he made the grade with *"him"* his knowledge did not matter; if he failed, it did not matter either… because the Spider would never live to leave the tunnels!

It was to the chamber which once had been the power plant of his home that the crooks took Wentworth. They knocked hesitantly upon a steel door. At a gentle command from inside, they thrust open the portal and ushered him through. Three chained wolves surged to their feet, but it was beyond them that Wentworth looked. Seated in a straight-backed, but otherwise comfortable, chair beneath a shaded light, a gray-haired man laid down a newspaper. He took off nose-glasses with the casual gesture of a householder about to address his butler. There was a stiff kindliness about this man's face until you looked into his eyes and they had a power and naked cruelty that was like the stab of a red-hot knife. It was the man who called himself Langdon Van Schlaick!

"Well?" he asked gently. "What news?"

Deferentially, one of Wentworth's captors spun the story of his arrival and, at the end, set down the bags of loot. Van Schlaick barely glanced at the greenback stuffed satchels, then his eyes came back to Wentworth's face.

"Very pleasant of you, I'm sure," he murmured, "though your purpose remains obscure. Why not have killed the man and taken the loot for yourself?"

Wentworth laughed jarringly, and kept the swagger of his poise, the jeering boldness of his eyes. "I may look like a fool, chief," he said flatly, "but my appearance has been known to deceive smart guys before this. If I'd figured I could get away with *his* loot, maybe I would have. From what I can see around this burg, it's safer, and more profitable to play ball with *'him!'* "

Van Schlaick nodded absently and Wentworth maintained his swaggering role, but his mind was questing furiously. Surely, this oldish man had neither the strength, nor the ambition to organize such a slaughter-mob as this; surely Van Schlaick was not… the *Butcher!*

"Yes, yes," the man murmured and shook out his paper preparatory to resuming his reading. "You are quite right, but I'm afraid the invitation to associate yourself with *'him'*—which I take it you seek—is a bit beyond the scope of my authority. Put him in the cell for the night, Oscar, until I've had a chance to consult *'him.'* "He peered over the paper for just an instant and a dry, stiff smile moved his bloodless lips. "Pleasant dreams, Death Hawkins."

Wentworth did not attempt to control the start that jerked at his muscles. "Geez, you know me then!" he gasped, in pretended admiration, then he resumed his swagger. "Okay. You know me. Then you know Death Hawkins isn't the kind to be shoved off in a cell. You let me see this *'him'* and we'll strike a deal just like that!"

Van Schlaick continued to smile as he turned his eyes back to the newspaper. He said nothing and Wentworth felt heavy hands clamp down on his shoulders. He started to resist, then gave in jauntily. The men wheeled him about toward the steel door.

"By the way," Van Schlaick called as the door slid shut. "You might feed the gentleman. He looks as if he might conceivably need nourishment."

THE CELL into which Wentworth was lowered presently was steel-lined and the entrance was a manhole cover that locked in place with a steel bar. Afterward, he heard the scrape of claws overhead and an eager snuffing about the cover and the grimness returned to his lips. He was secure against escape, all right. An oubliette for a prison, and ravenous wolves for a guard! Wentworth spent no time worrying about it. It was as good as promised that tomorrow he would meet *"him."*

Wentworth's face contorted with hatred despite a violent effort at control. When he was face-to-face with the Butcher of these thousands, there would be a reckoning! Even in that moment of premature triumph, Wentworth knew a hesitation, a faltering in his stern will. Suppose the Butcher proved to be... *Kirkpatrick!* Wentworth shook his head. No, it was impossible. Even insane, Kirkpatrick would not turn to such horror...

123

could not. Uncertainties shook him in his steel cell, but he did not permit it for long. He must gather strength for tomorrow's battle. Wentworth flung himself down on the quite comfortable couch that was provided and, by a strenuous effort of will, emptied his mind of all thoughts. He slept....

Wentworth's rest was deep, but it was the sleep of a man accustomed to emergencies. Every hour or so he roused and peered about him, listened to the snuffing of the wolves above—and slept again. After a long while, food was lowered to him, but the man, Oscar, volunteered nothing and Wentworth did not question him. He continued to rest through a period of hours, schooling himself against impatience and fears.

He was remembering now that Langdon Van Schlaick had addressed him by the name he had given in the abortive holdup of the saloon. That could mean only that information concerning the holdup had been relayed to him, and...Wentworth shrugged the bony width of his shoulders. It was a thing that must await his confronting of the Butcher.

Wentworth figured that it was close to eight o'clock the evening after he was confined, that Oscar removed the lid with an air of finality, though his broad, swarthy face was utterly blank. He tossed a box of clothing to Wentworth.

Oscar seemed to grudge speech. "Put them on. Half an hour."

He went away then, but the cover was not replaced, and presently there was a ring of wolf heads thrust over the rim—green eyes that regarded him implacably. Wentworth smiled grimly. The height of the ceiling, some five feet above his head, by no

means prevented the wolves from leaping down upon him...
but he thought they would not attack.

He opened the box and nodded at the fact that it contained
evening dress, complete to socks and the last stud. His eyes
were sharp, speculative, and he knew that the long rest had
profited him enormously. He could not believe that this clothing portended merely a meeting with the Butcher. *"He"* could
scarcely be so ceremonious. Then it must mean that he had been
accepted, at least for trial, as a member of the gang!

WENTWORTH RAPIDLY donned the clothing, found
that it fitted him remarkably well. He had just finished when the
wolves broke furtively away from the rim. After a brief showing
of Oscar's face, a rope ladder tumbled down into the oubliette.
Wentworth stood passively, a mocking grin on his face, and
made no effort to climb until Oscar gestured impatiently. He
was back in the role of Death Hawkins and he took his time
about climbing.

"What's the hurry, Oscar?" he drawled. "You need my room
for somebody else?"

Oscar grunted and gestured along the corridor. Wentworth
moved with a swaggering bravado, though his mind quested for
the answer of this treatment. If the Butcher were beyond that
steel door... but he could make no plans until he saw the man,
and what guards and weapons were available. No question of
what he would do if he had the opportunity, or could make one!

Imperturbably, Wentworth waited for Oscar to slide the steel
door aside. But when he strode inside, sharp disappointment
relaxed all his taut readiness. As on the night before, only Lang-

THE SPIDER

don Van Schlaick awaited him, seated rigidly in the straight-
backed chair. He rose immediately, glanced over Wentworth's
clothing with critical eyes.

"I see," he said gently, "that Wentworth's clothing fits you
very well indeed."

Wentworth gave no indication that the words meant anything
to him. "Wentworth?" he said. He grinned back at the stolid face
of Oscar. "You don't mean this punk, I can see that. He never
wore a soup and fish in his life."

Oscar seemed not to hear the words, and Wentworth turned
back to Van Schlaick with a shrug. Did this mean that Van
Schlaick had identified him, or had needed this clothing for a
final confirmation? Wentworth's posture seemed relaxed, but
he was counting the possibilities of escape. He would have to
dispose of Oscar first of all, and the man was powerful. It would
have to be a surprise attack, and....

"You have been investigated, Death Hawkins," Van Schlaick
continued mildly, "and I find you a man of some courage. Fool-
hardy, of course, like all your kind. Therefore, you are accompa-
nying me tonight as a bodyguard. Oscar?"

Oscar stepped forward, glowering, and handed Wentworth
his revolver. Wentworth laughed and weighed it on his palm,
snapped open the chamber and dumped the cartridges into his
hand. They were the right weight, he judged, and had not been
tampered with... but they were not explosive bullets. He rapidly
reloaded, thrust the revolver into his waistband.

"Okay, chief," he said. "Let's go. How about some cash? This
guy Wentworth didn't leave his pants pocket very well lined."

126

At Van Schlaick's gesture, Oscar returned to him the money and articles from his own clothing and there was no more conversation until they had threaded the tunnels and were seated in the rear of a chauffeur-driven landau, then Van Schlaick began to talk softly.

"Tonight, I am charged with the task," he said, "of snaring a traitor in our ranks. You... will help me."

Wentworth nodded carelessly and wondered if Van Schlaick meant to indicate him as the traitor. He would need to be bitterly alert tonight. He would learn what he could, but it was best to forget that he was Richard Wentworth and to enter wholeheartedly into the role of Death Hawkins. It was his ability to throw himself completely into another character that had made Wentworth such a master of disguise. He not only altered face and voice and gesture, he really became, for the time, the character into which he had poured himself. Death Hawkins undoubtedly would feel some anxiety, but he would cover it with his brazen swagger.

"Sure, chief," he agreed, "just show me the rat and I'll break him in bits for you."

"I know I can depend on you, Death," Van Schlaick nodded agreeably. "The difficulty is that we must trap also the person who has persuaded our man to become a traitor. You see, Death, we have been bothered lately by a plague."

"A plague?" Wentworth frowned. "I don't get you, chief."

"A plague," Van Schlaick nodded slowly, "of black spiders... or of one Black Widow Spider, to be more accurate. Tonight, we will... destroy her."

CHAPTER 9
TRAP FOR A TRAITOR

I T WAS hard to maintain the role of Death Hawkins after that—with the eyes of Langdon Van Schlaick sliding toward him in somber amusement from time to time. There seemed no possible doubt now that Van Schlaick was fully aware of his identity and yet his behavior was scarcely what would be expected of a criminal who had the Spider in his power. Too many men had attempted to triumph over that grim avenger, and the Underworld had learned that it was not safe to… play with him. Usually his identification was greeted by hysterical attempts to shoot him down on the spot!

There could be no doubt at all that Van Schlaick implied a trap had been set for Nita van Sloan. The thought sent a madness, like heat, through Wentworth's brain. Wasn't he playing the fool? Surely, this dried-up stiff old man beside him must be the Butcher himself! It would be easy to jerk out his revolver and take him prisoner, to kill the chauffeur if he resisted… but if he were wrong? Yes, precisely that was the difficulty. If he were wrong, and Van Schlaick were only a lieutenant as he indicated, then the Spider would have ruined his one strong chance to find and kill the man who was destroying the city!

So Wentworth continued to listen to the gliding, slow voice of Langdon Van Schlaick, talking now about things that did not matter. The limousine rolled its placid way through the city traffic to deposit them eventually at the marquee of a theater where a Broadway musical hit was playing. Van Schlaick handed Wentworth a ticket.

"You will be three rows behind me," he said quietly. "Presently an usher will come down and speak to me. When he leaves, you will follow and take him, and the woman to whom he speaks, as my prisoners. You will have help."

"I don't need help," Wentworth grinned brazenly.

"Yes," Van Schlaick agreed. "Of course not. However much I may be convinced of your ability, '*he*' made the plans for tonight. You understand?"

Wentworth wiped the smile from his lips. The death-like mask he had made of his face had a pallid glisten and it was hard to keep the fear out of his eyes... fear for Nita. So far, during the weeks' long domination of the Butcher, when "*he*" made the plans, they succeeded. This time, success meant... Nita's death!

"I get you, chief," he acknowledged and they filed through the crowd of chattering gay people about the theater entrance. There were many here whom Wentworth knew socially. It seemed to him that tonight their gaiety had a feverish note and men's faces had a grim cast. He caught fragments of phrases.

"Three thousand dead...."

"Awful. The roof just collapsed...."

"The police ought to do something...."

Wentworth knew he was hearing of the death that last night had stalked the Madison Square Garden, and the horror of it choked him. If he had needed anything to strengthen his determination, he had it now. This very night, he would drive through to the solution of this mad slaughter, no matter at what cost!

He lagged behind until Langdon Van Schlaick had taken his seat in a loge that was in the extreme front of the balcony, then he filed to a seat three rows behind him. He wanted desperately to look for Nita. But the search would be hopeless among these hundreds, more especially since she would not wish to be discovered. Moreover, there was the probability that men were watching him. He had a growing conviction that the trap for Nita would snap shut on himself as well. His hand stole, unconsciously, to press against the revolver at his waistband and his eyes burned on Van Schlaick's stiff, dignified head, a few feet before him.

THERE WERE two empty seats, one on each side of Van Schlaick, and these remained unoccupied until just after the curtain had lifted on the first act of the show. Then two men came quietly down the aisle with an usher and an oath leaped to Wentworth's lips. He could see only the men's silhouettes, but it was enough. That small, alert, quick-striding man in front, with the pompous challenge of his up-flung head, could be only Wilton Toley, district attorney for New York City! And that straight-backed colossus behind him, with his square head and its bristle of close-clipped hair, was Acting Police Commissioner Sanford Dane!

While a gust of laughter rocked the audience over the antics of the comedians on the stage, those two men filed in and sat on each side of Langdon Van Schlaick! Laughter, while these three leaned their heads together and began a whispered colloquy! Van Schlaick, who was at least the chief lieutenant of the Butcher, and the two men to whom these people had entrusted their defense against criminals… the head of the police, and the prosecutor!

Frantically, Wentworth sought for calmness. This meeting did not necessarily mean that Toley and Dane were involved with the criminals; not necessarily. Before this, the leaders of the Underworld had been on social terms with such officials and had managed to escape discovery. And yet it was strange.

Wentworth knew that Sanford Dane had been in the Great Store a short while before it had blown up, yet had escaped. He knew that Dane and Toley, both, were prizefight fans and would not ordinarily have stayed away from the championship bout the night before—yet they had not been destroyed in the wrecking of the arena. Those things *might* mean they had been forewarned, and were on friendly terms with the Butcher. It might mean one of them was… *the Butcher himself!*

Wentworth settled back grimly to wait and watch. He told himself that Van Schlaick might have wanted him to see this meeting, though that would presuppose definite knowledge of his real identity. Time would tell. He had been assigned a task to do, and in performing it he must snatch Nita from danger. What happened afterward would depend on many things….

It was midway of the first act that the usher walked slowly and unobtrusively down the aisle and stepped into the loge occupied by Van Schlaick and the two city officials. Van Schlaick twisted about in his seat so that Wentworth could see his face, could see the heads of the two men close together. The thin hand of Van Schlaick made a rather obvious business of passing a bit of folded paper to the usher.

132

The crowded theater instantly became panic-stricken!

Wentworth knew that was his signal and tautness crawled along his nerves. He had, suddenly, made up his mind what course to follow. He would take Nita prisoner! That way lay her surest protection. It would solidify his own position with Van Schlaick and enable him to make sure, once and for all, of the Butcher's identity. Afterward, he and Nita could break free together and strike back....

Wentworth acted with the thought. Before the usher turned away from Van Schlaick, Wentworth stepped out into the aisle and made his way slowly up the steps. At their head he paused a moment and the usher, moving swiftly, passed him and ran down the ramp toward the mezzanine lounge. Wentworth followed, keeping him in sight, watching intently for the "help" which Van Schlaick had promised. The lounge was deserted at this time, save for one other usher standing by the entrance to the men's room. But the man Van Schlaick had designated as a traitor strode directly toward the telephone booths.

Wentworth lighted a cigarette, quickened his stride and saw the man start into a telephone booth—and stop! He stopped with the suddenness of a bullet-struck animal, pulling up on his toes, bending forward at the waist with his momentum. Now Wentworth could see into the booth. He could see a woman's white hands! One of them held a snub-nosed automatic and the other was thrust out demandingly. Another stride and Wentworth could see her shoulders, her face... and it was completely concealed by a black mask! Nita! But he had known she would be here, hadn't he? And it was his plan to capture her.

WENTWORTH FLUNG a swift glance about him,

barely strangling the curse that rose to his lips. The help that Van Schlaick had promised was materializing. Damn it, he should have expected this from the fact that Toley and Sanford Dane were with the old man. The help were… *the police!* Three men in police blue had popped out of the men's room; another raised from behind a davenport. From one of the end ramps toward the loges and balcony, two other men in plain clothes were thrusting forward purposefully… and Nita wore a mask and had a gun in her hand!

In that swift moment, Wentworth recognized the whole of Van Schlaick's plan—of the Butcher's plan. Not only was he disposing of two enemies, but he was currying favor with the police by surrendering two much-wanted criminals. Nita had escaped involvement previously in the charges against Wentworth, but this action of hers finished all that. A black spider had been sprawled on the chest of the slain Manuel Lopez at the Club Angelic, and now… Wentworth's thoughts flashed across his brain even as he moved into action. He had given no indication to the police that he had spotted them. Now he strode calmly toward the booth where Nita held the usher at gunpoint.

The usher was trembling and his hand extended slowly, gripping the note that Nita obviously had demanded. As Nita's hand closed on it, the man's fist lashed out viciously! Nita's gun hand moved like lightning and the hard steel of the automatic smashed across the usher's knuckles. He uttered a choked cry, wheeled away… and Wentworth saw that only a portion of the note remained in Nita's hand.

"Hide!" Wentworth whispered.

135

He grabbed the usher by the collar and spun him into the second phone booth from Nita's. He seized the door and shoved it almost shut. "Stay there," he whispered. "I'm one of *his* men. Cops!"

An instant later, the police whipped about into the narrow corridor where the telephones were ranked. Guns were in their fists and there were scowls on their faces… the readiness to shoot. Wentworth had his back three-quarters turned toward them and he was lighting a cigarette. Nita opened the door of her booth and came out, smiling. Now he saw with relief that she had disguised face and hair.

"Everything was all right, wasn't it?" Wentworth asked easily.

Nita nodded brightly. "Yes, of course. Junior was asleep, but I can't help worrying, you know, and… Oh, look. What are those policemen doing here?"

Wentworth turned easily, funneling cigarette smoke from his nostrils; and one of the plainclothesmen thrust forward belligerently.

"Look," he said harshly. "An usher came in here."

Wentworth lifted his brows casually, "Did he really?" he asked. "I don't think I care for your tone of voice, officer. Come, dear, we'll miss the entire act if we don't hurry." He flicked his cigarette into a sand-filled jardiniere and offered his arm to Nita.

Nita glanced disdainfully at the police, put her hand on his arm. Wentworth could feel the slight tremor in it, but the police reluctantly fell aside and permitted them to pass. Nita began to talk, rapidly, through almost motionless lips.

"Dane and Toley went into Kirkpatrick's apartment tonight,"

she said. "I followed them here. Saw that old man with them give the usher a note. I have a part of it here." She glanced into her cupped palm, drew in a sharp breath. "I didn't get much of it. It simply says 'tonight!'"

Wentworth smothered a sharp exclamation. "We have to get the rest of that note!" He rapidly explained his own role and plan. "If I take you prisoner, you'll undoubtedly be arraigned before the Butcher himself. Then we'll have our chance. It's a heavy risk for you to take, dear, but...."

"I'm willing," Nita whispered. "Oh, anything to end this awful, terrible slaughter!"

"Just a minute, sir!" The voice called from behind, and Wentworth turned to see the detective striding toward him. "You won't mind showing me your ticket stubs, huh?"

Wentworth felt Nita's hand tighten on his arm and, as he turned slowly to face the detective, she flicked a stub out of her purse and pressed it into his hand. He had his own and he could easily palm Nita's and bring them out together. But it would not work, and he knew it. They would not show seats together. His mind raced furiously ahead.

"I know of no particular reason why I should," he said shortly. "What the devil do you mean by this, anyway? Commissioner Dane is here tonight. His seat is just a few rows ahead of ours. I think we'll go and have a talk with him and see if he wants his men disturbing taxpayers."

The detective's face was red, but the set of his jaw gave no sign of relenting. "That's all right, too, sir, but we had a tip that usher was going to be snatched. He walked into the place where you were, and disappeared...."

"And so you expect to pull him out of my pockets?" Wentworth smiled thinly. "Very well. I suppose I'll have to accommodate you."

He palmed Nita's stub and slipped his hand into his vest pocket, drew out the two together and extended them. At the same instant, there was a sharp cry from the direction of the phone booths. One of the policemen went back violently to the floor to the muffled echo of a pistol blast—and, gun in hand, the usher sprinted across the lounge toward Wentworth!

THE COP wheeled, clawing for his gun and Wentworth brought his left straight over to the jaw, straightening his well coördinated body behind the punch. The detective spilled to the floor and the usher, with a gasp of thankfulness, hurled himself into the ramp opening.

Nita tripped him neatly and, as he fell, Wentworth leaped back into the ramp opening—but, as he did, he whipped out his revolver and flung a shot above the heads of the police. They needed a few seconds of delay and he thought that would gain it. He heard, behind him, a few startled exclamations from the audience in the seats that flanked the ramp entrance, then Nita gasped.

He whirled to find the usher on his feet, charging wildly up the ramp. In that instant, he was lunging after the man, but Nita was beside him. "I couldn't find it," Nita wailed. "He played 'possum and then hit me...."

"Your mask!" Wentworth snapped. "He ruined your disguise."

Nita did not slacken her pace, but ripped the mask from her purse and hurriedly fastened it over her face as she ran.

He whirled.

They reached the head of the ramp and saw the usher charging full tilt down the middle aisle, past the seats of Van Schlaick and Dane and Toley. Commissioner Dane's huge body reared up against the lights of the stage. Men and women everywhere were jerking to their feet. They were not quite sure that this was something serious. It might be a surprise addition to the musical show, some new gag....

Beside Wentworth, Nita uttered a choked cry. The usher had reached the balcony rail, but did not check his pace. With a bound, he mounted the rail and plunged out into space!

For an instant, it looked like a hysterical suicide, but Wentworth immediately perceived the man's purpose. From the ceiling, there dangled a huge chandelier, studded with lights, and used as an electrician's bridge for stage spotlights. There were one or more men inside of it to handle the lights and there would be an exit through the ceiling. Even as the idea flashed across Wentworth's mind, the man's hands snared the edge of the chandelier. Wentworth saw at once, from the smoothness of the man's motions in the air, that he was a trained aerialist. His hands gripped the edge and his body swung forward beneath the chandelier. On the return, he heaved himself easily over the edge.

"Return to your seat," Wentworth whispered to Nita. "Chuck the gun and mask and change your disguise. I'll get this man!"

He wheeled and went sprinting, long-legged, across the width of the balcony. He knew the usual arrangement of the theater.

At the back of the boxes, that flanked the balcony and led up to the proscenium arch, there would be at least an iron ladder leading up into the area where the electricians' exit from the chandelier was located.

Guns began to slam as he raced, and he heard the shrill outbreak of panic among the audience. He did not glance back. He would need every second if he was to reach the exit of the chandelier before the fugitive. He knew that the note the man carried was of vital importance, and it had to be taken. There was more to this than police capture of himself and Nita; and obviously Van Schlaick had lied about the usher's tie-up with Nita.

A man's high vaulting scream rang out and Wentworth's head whipped about as he raced down the side aisle toward the boxes. From the forward edge of the chandelier a man's body was toppling! For an instant. Wentworth thought that it was the usher, then he saw that the man wore the overalls of an electrician. The man's scream bit off sharply as he plunged down among the audience, but a woman began shrieking in pain. The roar of guns was almost constant. There were powder-flashes stabbing out from the chandelier and… down the middle aisle of the balcony, Nita was running.

WENTWORTH STARED at her incredulously, then he realized what she was trying to do. She was shooting at the chandelier, attempting to prevent the usher from escaping before Wentworth should be able to intercept him! It was madness, but it was courageous madness. Never a thought of herself, as her few brief words to Wentworth had indicated. *Anything, oh anything, to end this awful slaughter….*

Even as Wentworth spotted her, he saw that the police were bursting from the entrance of the ramp. Their guns were in their hands, their eyes questing for a target. Wentworth saw one of the men point toward Nita and then others, with guns poised, were leaping at her. Sanford Dane was on his feet. There was a gun in his fist, too. Wentworth saw with a choking cry that the man was going to… was going to shoot Nita!

Wentworth's gun was in his hand, but even as he wrenched it about, he realized the futility of the gesture. He could not shoot at the police. If he could, there still would be too little time for him to drop all the men that threatened Nita. A mad laughter leaped to his lips.

With a long stride, he ripped down the velvet curtains of the nearest box and sprang to the rail of the box itself, poised over the audience pit. The drape whirled into the air and settled over his shoulders like a cape. Those shoulders no longer had the upright carriage of Richard Wentworth, nor the slouched swagger of Death Hawkins. They were crooked and bent as were the shoulders of the Spider, and it was the Spider's laughter that, flat and mocking, rang out through the theater!

"Flee, fools!" he cried. "Flee, before the theater is blown up! Flee, before the roof caves in like the roof of Madison Square Garden. Flee, while there is time!"

Every eye swung toward him. Leveled guns, poised to kill Nita—to check this mad chase through the crowded theater—swung toward the poised and crooked figure of the Spider upon the rail of the box. The audience rose to its feet as one man and a mad rush for the doors began… and then came the explosion!

Wentworth was jarred from his purchase upon the rail of the box, almost hurled to death below. For a crazy moment, he thought that his wild shout had hit on the truth, and that the building actually was collapsing. Then he saw the truth. The explosion had taken place up there in the chandelier. One of *"his"* explosive bullets. Even as Wentworth stared, the chandelier broke loose from its moorings in the ceiling and plunged down upon the milling hundreds in the audience below!

CHAPTER 10
THE GREATEST SACRIFICE

THROUGH A heart-breaking moment, Wentworth stood helpless while destruction whirled down upon the huddled human beings in the orchestra. But he could do nothing… *nothing*. Even as he realized the enormity of the thing that had happened, the heavy chandelier crashed to earth. Screams switched off and a powdering of dust floated airily upward. Afterwards, silence….

The police were still huddled about Nita over there in the middle aisle. She had been seized, captured. If they stripped off her mask….

"The ignorance of the police," Wentworth called mockingly, "is truly amazing. Run along and pick up the pieces."

A shout of anger volleyed up from the blue-coated men. In a breath, the bulk of the men were pounding toward Wentworth. Guns cracked in their fists. And yet, crouched under the velvet curtain he had made into a cape, Wentworth delayed. He saw one officer thrust Nita up the middle aisle toward the ramp... then he turned and fled. His swift mind already was at work. He had to snatch Nita from captivity, find Van Schlaick and convince him that Death Hawkins had fulfilled his duty.

He flung himself down the narrow passageway behind the boxes, spotted the steel ladder leading upward, and hurled bodily toward it. He was almost at the top when the police thundered into the corridor. Wentworth sent the velvet curtain swirling toward them, to confuse their aim. Then he dragged himself upward. A bullet punched through the ceiling within an inch of his head and another clanged off the iron of the ladder. But he was through the trap.

He slammed the door shut, threw a bolt into its sockets and instantly was running again. Over in the middle of the vast low room was a gaping hole that marked where the chandelier had been blasted loose. Wentworth paid it no heed. He sprinted, bent double, toward the front of the theater. There was a row of small decorative windows there, and the glass already was smashed from them by the concussion of the explosion.

Moments later, he was wriggling out. The electric sign, built at an angle from the facade of the theater, afforded him a perfect ladder. He went down swiftly while his eyes combed the windows of the building. He spotted those that would open into the second-floor lounge toward which the officer had been conducting Nita. Time was so precious. If Sanford Dane and Wilton Toley followed the cop, the mask would be torn from Nita's face. The fist of the usher already had made a wreck of her make-up and there would be no difficulty about recognizing her as Nita. He must save Nita from the hunted outlaw life he led.

He reached the sill of the curtain shrouded windows of the lounge and eased it up gently—stepping unseen to the floor in the protection of the velvet drapes. He parted them carefully and, through the crack, glimpsed the cop standing beside Nita a dozen feet away. The mask was still over her face but Sanford Dane's blocky powerful silhouette showed there in the entrance of the ramp. No time to delay! Wentworth slipped through the curtains and charged with long, swift bounds.

The impact of his feet startled the policeman. The man swung about, but Wentworth was too close for him to draw his gun. He attempted to dodge, struck out at Wentworth… and Nita struck him heavily behind the ear with the heel of a slipper snatched swiftly from her foot!

"The window," Wentworth gasped.

Nita went past him, running desperately. Sanford Dane was fumbling for a gun, directly beneath a glass-covered light that designated the entranceway. While he still fumbled, Wentworth whipped out his own revolver and fired. The bullet smashed into the glass, deluging Dane with fragments. He staggered backward, throwing up both arms, certain that he had been hit. Before he could recover, Wentworth, too, had flung himself violently at the window.

The street eddied with the thousand fleeing, panic-stricken people from the theater. Already it was jamming with taxicabs and mounted police. For the moment, their flight through the window would not seem spectacular… if they could achieve it before Sanford Dane bawled orders through the window! Wentworth swept Nita to the edge of the marquee, helped her climb over the sign that lifted like a barrier. From there, it was an easy leap to the top of a taxi. Wentworth was beside her when they heard a shout from the window. Dane could not see them, nor could people in their immediate vicinity see Dane.

WENTWORTH CLIMBED to the ground and helped Nita down. They merged with the crowd while mounted police tried to force their way nearer through the stampede. "Get home as fast as you can, dearest," Wentworth ordered, "and for heaven's sake, keep out of this fight."

Nita's hand was clinging to his arm and he could feel the weakness and trembling of his own body. She could sense it, too. The last few strenuous moments had drained him terribly. He was panting harshly, his forehead glistened with the perspiration of weakness.

"I'm going to find Van Schlaick's car," he said hoarsely. "I'll be waiting for him when he comes back. If he suspects me, it's the end of Van Schlaick. Otherwise…."

"Otherwise?" Nita prompted softly.

Wentworth shook his head. "That message said something was going to happen tonight. It may well be another tragedy like that Madison Square Garden business. I've got to find out!"

"That's how I figured it," Nita nodded. "I'm going with you!"

Wentworth tried to stop in the press of the fleeing crowd, but could not. Nita pressed close to him.

"Don't you understand, Dick?" she whispered. "It is more important than ever now that you convince Van Schlaick of your

145

loyalty. Without that, he will never confide in you. How better can you prove that to Van Schlaick than by obeying his orders! By bringing me in a prisoner!"

Wentworth got his shoulders against the brick wall of a building and pulled Nita into the eddy behind him. "Don't you understand, dear," he whispered. "Van Schlaick only wants you to kill you! You can't run that risk!"

Nita smiled up into his face and tenderness was in her eyes. "You talk to me of risks, Dick? You who deliberately drew the fire of the police…" Her voice broke. "Dick, forget you and me. This is the one way that we can learn what is planned for tonight!"

It was an accident that forced Wentworth's hand. He saw Van Schlaick's car and, even as he spotted it, the chauffeur turned his head and saw him. Wentworth clamped his hand on Nita's arm. "All right," he muttered. "Keep your gun and hide it. You're right. We have no right to think of ourselves—only of smashing this hellish conspiracy."

He was silent then while Nita began to struggle against his grip. He thrust her the last ten feet toward the car, grasped the rear door and shoved her inside.

"Hell-cat!" he snarled. "Now you stay put, or I'll slug you again!" He leaned forward to throw swift words at the chauffeur. "The cops tried to grab her off after the chief told me to snatch her. If cops come out with the chief, you'd better get away from here fast and send another car for him."

"Cripes, yes," the man grunted. "I ain't taking no chances with the coppers."

But Wentworth's precautions in that direction were unnecessary for when Van Schlaick pushed through the crowd he was alone. He sprang nimbly into the back of the car and then stiffened sharply, clawed out a gun!

Wentworth said sharply, "Hey, chief, what's the matter? It's just me and the dame you told me to grab off. You should of told me the cops were going to try for her, too. I had a hell of a time getting her away from them."

Van Schlaick stood as erectly as possible, head bowed against the pressure of the roof, gun still in his hand. Then slowly he smiled his stiff-lipped way and shoved the revolver back into its holster.

"You surprised me, Death Hawkins," he said gently. "Allow me to congratulate you on your success. You have actually captured the Black Widow."

Wentworth shrugged, twisting around to glare at Nita. "I don't know anything about that, but the dame can certainly sting. This is the one that was taking the paper away from the usher. But say, chief, that usher didn't seem to be in cahoots with her. He didn't want to give up the paper."

Van Schlaick selected a cigar from a case in his pocket, trimming it with exquisite small movements of his long hands.

"I'm afraid," he said softly, "that the problem can hold only academic interest now. The usher is dead. You, however, have served me well, Hawkins. I shall see that 'he' knows of it and that you are properly rewarded. Yes, indeed, I always like to see energetic and enterprising young men properly rewarded."

NOTHING ELSE was said until they had threaded the traffic and made their way once more through the corridors beneath the earth. Nita marched stolidly before them under the muzzle of the chauffeur's gun. Wentworth was motioned to follow her into Van Schlaick's room and, the instant he stepped across the threshold, the door slid solidly shut behind him.

He wheeled, but the door was already locked tight. His hand flicked to the gun at his waist and he swore softly. Sometime in the car, Van Schlaick had succeeded in removing the gun! Nita was facing him, her lips open for speech, but Wentworth waved her to silence.

"Hey, chief," he yelled. "Hey, what the hell?"

There was no answer at all through the thickness of the steel. Wentworth's eyes quested over the room. Everything was as he had last seen the place, except for one thing. On a liqueur cabinet against the far wall stood a thick green bottle with a buff-colored label. Wentworth moved toward it and, when he saw the label, his lips drew thinly together.

"Your sacrifice was useless, Nita," he said gently.

Nita moved swiftly to his side, "How do you know?" she asked softly. "Are you sure he isn't listening."

Wentworth lifted his shoulders slowly and nodded toward the thick green bottle. The label read, *Pernod Fils—Absinthe.*

"Presently," he said steadily, "Van Schlaick will let his wolves in here. That absinthe will turn them back, a secret which one Blinky McQuade, whom Van Schlaick knows to be the Spider—has used once before. When I use the absinthe, he will be sure."

"Then don't," said Nita softly, "use the absinthe."

"It does not matter," Wentworth shrugged. "He is merely tantalizing us. He knows."

"*He?*"

Wentworth wheeled to face Nita alertly. "You think that Van Schlaick is the Butcher?"

Nita smiled. "Van Schlaick, or Wilton Toley, or Sanford Dane, or Stanley Kirkpatrick."

"Or you or me," Wentworth finished. He laughed, and the sound was bitter. "May I mix you a drink, ma'amselle?"

Nita nodded, graciously. "I think I should like a Pernod." She moved close to him and they laughed together as he mixed the drink. Under the cover of the sound, Nita whispered. "I have my gun, still with four shells in it."

His mind swiftly reviewed the situation.

"Dick…" Nita's voice was faint, uncertain. He wheeled toward her, found her swaying on her feet. "No, not the drink," she whispered. "Gas, I think. I…."

She pitched forward and would have fallen had not Wentworth's quick arms caught her. He tried to ease her to the floor and… he was on his knees. He swore, tried to struggle to his feet. Futile. This then was how Van Schlaick had trapped them. Damnable. With his final effort. Wentworth caught up the bottle of absinthe and overturned it on the floor beside them. If the wolves came….

WHEN WENTWORTH struggled back to consciousness, he realized that he was on his feet and that the sly, malicious voice of Langdon Van Schlaick was sounding in his ears.

"Come, come, Spider," he said cheerfully. "Surely, a little whiff of gas cannot extinguish your senses for these long hours? Nita came out of it much more quickly, I assure you."

Wentworth pried open his eyes and stared drunkenly about the room. The scene had not changed during his unconscious-ness except for one thing. Nita was gone, and in her place were a half-dozen armed men flanking Van Schlaick!

Wentworth tried to lift a hand to his forehead and there was an intolerable weight dragging at his wrist. Uncertainly, he stared down, saw that chains, with great balls of metal attached, were fastened to his wrists and ankles. In bewilderment, he saw something else. A long black cape was draped about his shoul-ders and his head… He glanced upward. Yes, a black hat had been drawn down over his brows. A thin smile drew back his lips. So they had decked him in his uniform to destroy him! The uniform of the Spider!

Wentworth put his eyes upon the implacable gaze of Van Schlaick. "I suppose this, too, is '*his*' idea?" he asked imperturb-ably.

Van Schlaick answered his smile. "As a matter of fact, it isn't, but I'm sure it will have approval. You see, Spider, we have another small mission to perform tonight. And we are going to allow you the privilege of leading us, in full costume."

"Nice of you," Wentworth murmured.

"You see," Van Schlaick was explaining, "nearly every enter-prise in the city is now paying us for our protection. There remains however, as '*he*' pointed out to me, the fact that we are receiving no fees from the hotels. Tonight, we bring them into line."

Van Schlaick nodded pleasantly, "I'm glad you're feeling better. Now, that you can understand, I will explain where Nita is. We knew it would be her wish to go with you, so we have sent her on ahead. She is on the roof of the hotel, similarly decorated with chains. She may not be too comfortable, since her couch is made up of a number of boxes of our very best explosive. But she won't be uncomfortable long. The explosives will be touched off from a neighborhood roof by one of our unpatented bullets. When Nita... goes off... the hotel will collapse very neatly and we shall begin collections!

"As usual," he said, "we will rob the till before we blow up the building. That is where you come in, Spider. You will go with us and direct the robbery. When it is over, unfortunately, you will be left behind. Our exit will be the signal for the blast. I trust you understand fully?"

"Fully," Wentworth said flatly.

He made no move, but suddenly three men were clinging to his arms and a gun ground into his back.

Van Schlaick smiled but made no other answer and the men thrust Wentworth forward across the room, through the long underground corridors. Wentworth was forced to walk bent almost double in order to lift the heavy weight that otherwise would have prevented him from walking. He staggered, feigning even greater weakness. He had no definite plan in mind, but always it was wise to conceal strength.

TWO CARS sped almost silently through the city, to draw to a halt at the side entrance of the Maté Hotel. It filled an entire city block and taxis lined the curb for two blocks beyond. They prevented any other traffic from breaking through to the hotel... but the line parted for the cars that contained the Butcher's men!

Wentworth's lips thinned with the knowledge that the taxi drivers must also be party to the crime that impended. Perhaps the men who regularly drove them had been killed; perhaps their cabs had been brought in... It did not matter. It was enough that there was this huge, mobile barricade which could block pursuit or facilitate the escape of criminals.

The two cars checked at the curb and, from the darkness, four cabs rolled up to form a blockade behind which their movements would go unobserved. Among them, Wentworth moved to a side entrance of the hotel, through a narrow corridor where a surprised bell-boy was crushed down with a single blow... and so to the door of the manager's office.

When the door opened, Wentworth was thrust violently forward so that he pitched to the floor, but if the criminals had expected any ambuscade, they were wrong. The manager and an assistant looked up from a survey of books and a half-dozen men wedged in with guns in their fists.

Van Schlaick stepped in last of all.

"Sorry to trouble you, gentlemen," he said gently. "I'll ask you to surrender all of your cash. One of my men will accompany your assistant to the till. The safe, I perceive, is already open and ready for us. That is pleasant of you!"

The manager surged, white-faced, to his feet. "Yes, yes," he stammered. "Take the money, but for God's sake...."

"For God's sake, don't blow up the hotel?" Van Schlaick asked softly. "I'm afraid that also will be necessary. Oscar, you will accompany the gentleman for the cash. Henry...."

The assistant manager stumbled as he left the room with the man called Oscar at his side. The other gunman, Henry, stepped toward the manager. His right arm moved with jagged force and the manager was hammered sideways to the floor. Henry bent over and his back arched, his shoulders swayed with the violence of his blows. He struck twice more with a short length of pipe.

The murder had taken place so swiftly that Wentworth had not even guessed at the meaning of the order to Henry—before it was executed. Then it was too late. He lay, hunched forward on his face, as if exhaustion had destroyed him, but he was gathering his forces. No one was paying any attention to him and very considerately they had supplied him with weapons. They had put balls of metal on his wrists.

Van Schlaick once more said, "Henry."

The killer turned away from his victim, his face twisted and white with blood-lust and his eyes sought out Wentworth. So that was the way it was to be! Wentworth pushed up on his knees.

"No, no," he gasped. "Not that way. Oh, God, don't kill me that way!"

Van Schlaick glanced down at him with a sardonic amusement and—Wentworth struck!

His two hands, gripping up short the chained ball weight on his wrists, chopped to the left—and Van Schlaick screamed and pitched forward on his face! His whole body contorted with agony, and Wentworth's eager hands snatched the old man's revolver in mid-air. Other gunmen were wheeling toward him, but Wentworth's first bullet smashed into the chest of the man, Henry!

The blast of that shot was devastating. Where Henry had stood, there were only fragments, and others in the room reeled drunkenly or fell to their knees under the impact of the shock. Wentworth picked, deliberately, two other targets and twice more pulled the trigger. There was nothing else in the room that could be called human, save Van Schlaick screaming on the floor and the gaunt length of the Spider heaving himself up to his full height.

Once more, Wentworth fired as Oscar lunged in through the door. Wentworth turned heavily back the way he had come. His feet dragged their heavy weights more easily on the polished floors, but he moved with the deliberation of an automaton.

THERE WERE screams in the lobby, and the excited shouts of men. The building was full of people and, at any moment, the bullet that would destroy the building might be fired. 'Destroy the building... and *Nita!* Wentworth's face was gray when he floundered into the lobby. He leaned into the small room containing the telephone exchanges.

"The building is going to be blown up," he said quietly. "Within a few minutes, I'm afraid. Call all the people in the building and get them out as swiftly as possible. Start with the top floors. Then call the police. Understand?"

The girls stared at him with frightened eyes, then one of them whispered her recognition of the garb and the distorted hunch of the shoulders. She announced it with a scream.

"The Spider. My God, the Spider! Yes, sure, we'll warn them. Right away. The police have already been called."

Wentworth went on toward the elevators. The starter tried to run, but the muzzle of Wentworth's gun transfixed him. "You will run the elevators as swiftly as possible," he said. "One floor at a time. Send them all to the top floor, then to the next to the top and so on. No stops once the cages have been filled. This building is going to blow up and you are going to get the people out, or I'll come back and kill you."

The elevator shot upward. Wentworth was trembling under the dragging weight of his chains, under the violent exertions required to move them. He was trembling, too, from the strain that tore at his heart. Van Schlaick had said that their exit from the hotel would be the signal for the explosion on the roof. If they did not make that exit… Wentworth clamped his jaw tightly. He might have made sure of reaching Nita in time, by not giving warning below. There was even some justification for it, since the explosives which would fell the building were on the roof, and if he could reach them….

The elevator boy was staring at him, his whole body shaken by trembling. Wentworth's lips relaxed in a slight smile. "You have no need to fear me," he said quietly. "No honest man has. Get the people down as fast as you can. Hurry them. It is the only hope."

Wentworth dragged out into the corridor and people shrank back against the walls, then darted into the elevator he had left. They were not waiting to dress, he saw, and was encouraged. If they would all take the orders seriously, they might yet be saved.

Wentworth was hurrying toward the doorway that would

take him up a final flight of stairs to the roof; hurrying, dear God, at the pace of a snail! He looked down at the revolver in his hand, clicked open the chamber. Two more cartridges. He had reached the door, and wrenched at the knob. It refused to open! Wentworth swore, stepped back, leveled his revolver—but did not fire!

Dear God, if he fired now, he might very easily set off the whole charge of explosives upon the roof!

The window was open. He leaned over the sill and gazed upward. There were regular, narrow ledges leading upward to the two-foot shelf of the gutters. That, then, was the way he must go. He clambered heavily over the sill, looked down at the weights upon feet and wrists and the smile that wrenched at his lips was twisted with despair.

It would be a man's size job for him to climb that wall in his weakened condition, even without this handicap. Weighted down as he was, it was an impossibility. Well, he had survived and triumphed through the performance of the impossible! For the Spider, there could be no such word! Wentworth gripped the revolver between his teeth, swung his weighted feet to the ledge and, painfully straightened to his task.

He heard a man shout. He peered warily across the canyon of the street and saw the man. He was leaning over the edge of the opposite roof and he gripped a revolver in his hand. As Wentworth stared, the man fired... and the bullet blasted dust from the rocks beside Wentworth's face! White-faced, Wentworth gripped his revolver. If he fired... If he fired, the concussion of the explosive bullet might bring this entire hotel building down in ruins about him!

Wentworth realized that he had no choice. He must shoot. The only thing he could do would be to place his bullet where the force of the explosion that followed would be muffled as much as possible. The building was sixty feet away.

He watched the man crouch low and steady his gun across his forearm. Wentworth leveled his own revolver across his chest, pulled the trigger. The recoil almost unbalanced him, and the instant concussion of the explosive bullet tugged at him with fiendishly clever hands. He clung to the wall… and saw there was no longer a gunman leaning over the parapet across the street. Laboriously, Wentworth took the gun between his teeth once more and began to climb. Each upward lift of a hand dragged pounds of metal weight with it; his feet were tons-heavy.

Seconds dragged themselves into long minutes and their trickling past was added weight on his wearied body, on his despairing soul. When he reached the out-thrust shelf of the two-foot eave, he was close to exhaustion. Perspiration made gleaming rivulets across his temples and the hand he stretched out to grip the edge of the eave was shaking uncontrollably.

With the strain of these weights, he couldn't quite make it. Wentworth's lips set grimly and he deliberately swung the weights until their momentum jerked them up over the rim. After that, he could get his fingers over the cave. It took the last ounce of his strength to draw his body up over the shelf and afterward he lay there sobbing the breath into his lungs.

He drove himself to his feet. He had killed one of the armed guards, perhaps the one who was charged with setting off the explosives. He could not be sure. Another might come. Laboriously, he climbed the parapet and a glad cry greeted him. Bound to a heaped pile of boxes and cans, Nita was stretched out helpless in her ropes.

"Oh, Dick," she cried. "Oh, Dick I knew you would come, I knew it. But quickly, before this stuff… is set off."

Far below, in the street, there was a faint rising murmur that he knew was the sound of panic-stricken, fleeing human beings. How far had the emptying of the hotel progressed? He could not tell. Seconds, or hours might have passed since he left the elevator. His hands fumbled with the ropes that bound Nita and there was no strength in his fingers. He groped in his pockets, found a small pocket-knife and hacked at the hemp.

As soon as she could stagger to her feet, she began to tear down the pile of explosives and scatter the boxes close against the brick parapet so that no searching bullet could find them.

"Lie still," Nita told him softly. She ran toward him with a powdered substance from one of the cans of explosive. "Put your ankle chains across this," she ordered and heaped the powder into a close pile. An instant later, a spurt of hot blue flame flared up from the stuff as she touched a match to it. Three times she repeated the action and Wentworth could feel the heat working along the chain to his ankles. He stared curiously, and saw that the steel was white hot! Two more bursts of the burning powder, and the chain fell in two halves, the weight lay upon the roof.

"Now your wrists," Nita said quietly. "There was thermite, too."

A grim smile touched Wentworth's lips. He knew now. Kirkpatrick. His friend held the answer, either in guilt or innocence. Wentworth pushed to his feet. The release of the weights made him feel spry and light. He smiled down into Nita's upturned face, rested his hands lightly on her shoulders.

"The end is near, dear. We must get out of this hotel, and then…."

"And then?" Nita prompted.

"Why, I will keep my promise and visit you at your apartment, dear. You must go and wait for me." His jaw hardened beneath his smile and the light in his gray-blue eyes turned cold. "I won't be long."

"Oh, Dick, not again!" Nita flung herself close into his arms and, at the same moment, the crash of an ax biting into an armored door echoed sullenly across the roof. Nita flinched and turned toward the sound.

"That," Wentworth said flatly, "will be the police. I'm afraid that, even after this, there will be no amnesty for the Spider. Lie down, I'll tie you up again. That will give you an alibi."

In a few deft gestures, he bound Nita and bent to kiss her before he fled toward the parapet. The ax blows were fast and furious now, the door weakening. It must mean that the hotel was cleared, or else that the police, too, had word that the explosives were on the roof. No matter, now. In a few moments, the police would be up here and, after that, there would be no chance of the explosives being set off. Nita would tell them….

Wentworth groped for the narrow ledges by which he had climbed, found them and went swiftly down the wall. As he had told Nita, it was like flying to be rid of the chains. He descended two stories before he dared try a window, and then he crossed swiftly through a deserted room to the hall door. The sound of ax-blows had ceased. Wentworth nodded to himself. He tossed the Spider cape and hat through the window, stepped into the hall. As he raced down the steps, he also discarded his suit coat, collar and tie.

He had almost reached the front door of the hotel when the gates of an elevator slammed open and the shouts of police burst out in his wake.

"Stop him!" they shouted. "Stop him, he's the Spider!"

WENTWORTH RECOGNIZED the hoarse voice of Sanford Dane, the police commissioner! Wentworth's hand touched the gun in his shirt and the smile turned grim on his mouth. This was as it should be. Let them follow him to Kirkpatrick's apartment!

Wentworth plunged into the welcome shadows that skirted the building, doubled the corner toward Lexington Avenue. Already, his heart was pounding in his throat, breath brassy in his mouth. A gun slammed behind him, but he heard no whine of lead. Then there was the rapid pound of running feet.

Wentworth did not check his speed in the slightest degree. But ten feet from the policemen who were braced to stop him, he sprang forward in what appeared a headlong tackle. Then his hands touched the ground and he performed a powerful handspring that sent him in a graceful somersault over the confused

160

heads of the two police. Before they could collect themselves, he had plunged into the crowd. Dane's shouted words aided him here, for the ranks parted in fear and, moments later, Wentworth sprang to the running-board of a fire-department pumper.

He quickly wrenched the truck into gear, twisted the tail of the siren, and sent the truck lurching forward. Men and women stumbled from his path. There was a brief check as the short length of hose to the fire hydrant drew taut, then the cast-iron plug broke off at its base and water geysered into the air.

The truck gathered frantic speed and the crowds spilled from its path. The siren shriek was deafening and Wentworth kept the howler going full blast. He was straightening away up Lexington Avenue and it was fully two minutes before the first of the police cars swung out on his trail. Let them follow!

IT WAS less than ten minutes after he had stolen the fire truck that Wentworth yanked it to a halt in front of an apartment house on Park Avenue and leaped past the startled doorman and into the lobby. The elevator boy started to shut the doors then caught the fierce gleam of Wentworth's eyes and did not.

"Up!" Wentworth snapped at him. "Eighteenth floor!"

He stopped the cage, flung wide the door with a flourish and Wentworth motioned him back down. For a long moment, he stood there motionless while his eyes searched the empty corridor. At one end was a fire-exit; the other end was a blank wall, and Wentworth remembered that there was another apartment building there. He nodded and went quietly to the door of Kirkpatrick's apartment. Once more the pocket knife came skillfully into use and the lock yielded. Wentworth stepped into Kirkpatrick's apartment!

"Where are you, Kirk?" he called quietly then. "It's Dick."

His voice ran along the empty corridor and then light sprang up in Kirkpatrick's bedroom and Kirkpatrick's voice came wearily to his ears, "In here, Dick. Come in."

Wentworth nodded and swung in through the doorway, reached the foot of the bed in two long strides and stopped there. His right shoulder was thrust a little forward and, at his entrance, his eyes had made a swift canvass of the room. Empty, of course; empty except for the gaunt frame of Kirkpatrick, stretched out upon the bed. And there was no welcome in Kirkpatrick's saturnine, drawn face. A long-barreled revolver was in Kirkpatrick's right hand.

"So you've come for me, Dick?"

Wentworth nodded lightly. "Exactly, Kirk. And the police are right behind me. You might as well wait until they arrive to make your confession."

There was a wildness in Kirkpatrick's eyes that did not belong there and they burned into Wentworth's with an eager flame, as if he were trying to convey some message; some appeal.

"Dick," he whispered. "Dick, you were a fool to come here."

Wentworth nodded and the lift of his eyebrows was quirky. "I know it, Kirk. You see, I had to tell you in person. I was telling Nita that I wouldn't believe you were the Butcher, even if you confessed it with your own lips. I want to test myself."

Perspiration was standing out on Kirkpatrick's forehead. "Dick, think what you're saying," he whispered. "Think...."

He was interrupted by the tramp of heavy feet in the hallway and, an instant later, Sanford Dane and Wilton Toley slammed into the room behind Wentworth. They jerked to a halt and Dane's heavy voice boomed out.

"Thank God we got here before this murdering scoundrel…."

Wentworth smiled and did not look toward them, but kept his eyes on Kirkpatrick. "I was just telling Kirk," he said quietly, "that even his own confession would not make me believe him the Butcher."

"Kirkpatrick… the Butcher!" Dane stammered.

Kirkpatrick's long-barreled gun was pointing past Wentworth at the two men behind him. "You will drop your guns, gentlemen," he said coldly. "At once!"

Dane stammered. "What the hell is this?"

"Drop them!" Kirkpatrick's voice leaped out in command. "That's better. Now then, come closer so that you can hear what I am about to say, and don't attempt any foolishness. There are explosive bullets in this gun."

"Explosive bullets!"

Kirkpatrick said savagely, "Damn it, stop repeating me! Listen. I framed Wentworth for the murder of Fritz Street. He isn't guilty and I can alibi him. As for the rest… Dick, tell them why you came here."

Wentworth said, "Certainly."

His eyes swung sideways and, with the help of a mirror over a dresser, he could see the end wall of the room perfectly. He began to go over it, inch by inch, as he talked, relating the phone call a man had made to an extortionist—but did not mention that it had been Manuel Lopez who had called Kirkpatrick's number and used Kirkpatrick's name. He mentioned the hidden garage, and the death trap that had been set in it. Kirkpatrick's face took on a rigid pallor, but the gun in his hand was unswerving.

"Then, too," Wentworth continued placidly, "there was the fact that you two gentlemen, Toley and Dane, went directly from this apartment to a conference with a man I know to be the lieutenant of the Butcher, one Langdon Van Schlaick. You probably arrested him, his legs broken, in the Maté Hotel, did you not?"

"Van Schlaick?" rumbled Dane. "Certainly not.

He wasn't in the hotel, and I wouldn't have arrested him anyway. He was my father's friend and there never was a more upright man. It was through his help that we almost caught the Spider at the theater last night."

"I radioed to Doctor Smithers, who was in charge of Kirk," Wentworth continued more softly. "Smithers said that Kirk had escaped from him at Shanghai and that he thought Kirk was out of his mind. The truth is, isn't it, Kirk, that you had just heard of the accusation against me and flew back to give me the alibi that only you could supply?"

Kirkpatrick shook his head. There were circles of fatigue beneath his eyes. "No," he said thickly. "I came back to finish my work. You fools, I am the Butcher, and you shall not escape alive from this room!"

WENTWORTH'S EYES were motionless now and he had found what he sought. There was a silhouette of Kirkpatrick's profile hung on the wall. It was the only black spot on that entire expanse, and it was a curious thing that something as dead black as a silhouette should show a glint of light. Wentworth drew in a slow breath and leaned forward a little over the foot of the bed. He beat the palm of his right hand on the wood and his left slipped inside his shirt to the grip of his revolver.

"Kirkpatrick," he said, "you're lying. You're lying to protect our lives because…."

He had leaned forward far enough and his unerring instinct for marksmanship told him that the revolver muzzle was pointed at the silhouette upon the wall. If he was wrong, they were all dead men! If he was wrong… Wentworth interrupted his words and squeezed the trigger. Powder flame burned his chest and he felt a searing touch beneath his right arm as the bullet sped past and, even as he felt those things, he was hurled violently to the floor by an explosion.

He was rolling as he hit, scrambling up beside the bed, placing his body between Kirkpatrick and the wall at which he had fired and then triumph crowded a hard laughter up into his throat. For he saw that the bricks of the wall lay on the floor of Kirkpatrick's room, and that meant the explosion had occurred on the other side of the wall. It meant that his bullet had sped true and… he had killed the Butcher!

Dane and Toley picked themselves up from the floor and stared in amazement at what the hole torn in the wall revealed. Sprawled upon the floor, kicking out the last throbs of his life, was the corpse of a man, and there were three chained wolves dead upon the floor. Only by the rusty, old-fashioned clothing, and by the fragments of the hair was the man identifiable, but it was enough. It was Langdon Van Schlaick!

"Fingerprints will identify him for you," Wentworth said swiftly, "and Kirkpatrick will confirm the story and convict him… convict his memory for you. Kirkpatrick was a prisoner here in his own home, and Van Schlaick played at being his own lieutenant, but he aimed, in the end, to lay all the blame at Kirkpatrick's door. When his plan at the hotel fell through, he knew that he was beaten unless he could destroy me, and make you two think that Kirkpatrick was guilty. This was his last, most desperate play. I think you'll find the mechanism of a secret doorway cut through the wall there, and that information from Kirkpatrick's secret files was used."

Kirkpatrick lay back on the pillows, relaxed, and there was a grave smile on his lips. "What Mr. Wentworth tells you, gentleman, is the exact truth, and I can give you proof. There was little enough I could do, but I rigged cameras and dictographs to record Van Schlaick's conversations. He would have killed you all if I had not talked as I did."

Dane and Toley were walking heavily toward the doorway and, suddenly, Dane wheeled toward Kirkpatrick. "This is all very pretty, and I'll admit you're not the Butcher, Wentworth," he said heavily. "But there is still the matter of the thirty-seven police who were killed around your house by an explosion you set off, and…."

Wentworth reached the door in a long jump, slammed and locked it from the outside, then he ran lightly along the hallway, He ran unevenly and twice, as he hurried, he stumbled and had to catch himself against the wall. There was a smile on his lips, but heaviness was in his breast. He had hoped to smash the case against himself at the same time he destroyed the Butcher and he was still a homeless, hunted man. Wilton Toley would not forget the indictment.

Wentworth laughed softly as he ran, took the steps downward. Well, he would not grieve. This way, Nita was safer, and his enemies would have more trouble finding him. Living in the Underworld, as he would, he could discover the machinations of new criminal leaders even earlier, and strike more swiftly. Wentworth realized that the Spider was entering a new and perilous stage of his life. It would be hard to lose the happiness of Nita's comfort and nearness, but it would be safer for her that way. And he could occasionally pay her a visit, such as he had promised her tonight.

HE WAS on the twelfth floor and he punched the bell lightly, three times. An instant later, the door was flung wide and Nita ran into his arms. At each side of the portal, stood one of his sturdy men, Ram Singh and Jackson.

"The Butcher is dead," Wentworth told them quietly, "but Dane is still after me for the deaths of various police. I'm afraid it won't be possible to stay very long."

Nita's smile grew strained. "The Fritz Street case?"

Wentworth told her rapidly about Kirkpatrick. "I knew Kirk couldn't be guilty and I knew, too, that after the last failure, the Butcher would try to pin the crime on him. Then, too, all this evidence pointing toward Kirk and Kirk's apartment indicated a hideout there. That was how I happened to spot the gunport in the wall. Well, forget that. I am paying you a formal call, Miss van Sloan."

Nita laughed and presently, Ram Singh brought him fresh clothing. He excused himself to dress and, when he returned, there was a dinner spread and Nita led him to a table nearby, where she indicated a violin case with a gift card on it.

"It can't come up to your Stradivarius, Dick," she said, "but it was the best I could find… and I knew you'd miss your violin most of all the things that were destroyed in your home."

Wentworth opened the case and smiled across it at Nita, gathered her suddenly, strongly into his arms. It was at that moment that there was a heavy pounding at the door and he heard Dane's voice.

"You can't get away, Wentworth, the house is surrounded!"

Nita laughed, for all that there was a catch in her throat. "That's what he thinks!" she said. "My window opens on the level of the roof to the south. On the north, there is a doorway cut through the wall into the next building and I have rented the apartment that adjoins it next door. There are a hundred disguises in a secret dressing-room there. Take your choice, Dick—and, oh, my lover, come back soon!"

Wentworth bent to her waiting lips, then caught up the violin case. "The adjoining apartment, I think, Nita," he said.

Nita told him rapidly, and Wentworth ducked through the door while Nita went to let in the police. Sanford Dane was in a rage, and thundered at her.

"Wentworth might as well surrender," he shouted. "He has

to face trial for those police deaths, no matter how many alibis Kirkpatrick can give him for the Street affair."

Nita smiled mockingly up into the craggy face of the acting police commissioner. "Why, whatever makes you think Mr. Wentworth is here?" she asked. "He would be welcome, of course."

"He can't get away. The building is surrounded!"

Nita shrugged and moved carelessly across the room. She took up a cigarette.

"Ram Singh," she said, "you may allow the police to search, but see that they don't steal anything—or plant anything."

She went to the window and there was no indication in her graceful poise of the tension that rippled through her every nerve. Dick was clever, yes, but he was weary and the police were on every side. They... Her thoughts broke off. Faint with distance, she could catch the strains of a violin, played by a master's hand. It lilted in a serenade and, bending forward slightly, Nita could see the hunched figure of a crippled musician, playing his instrument on the street below. Nita laughed with the sudden relief.

"Make sure, Jackson," she called, "that the police see *everywhere*. It really was time that I got a bit of rest."

She pulled the window down slowly, and drew the shade, as a signal to Dick that she had heard—but even then it seemed to her that she could hear the sweet strains of the violin, soft as love words whispered in her ear.

POPULAR HERO PULPS AVAILABLE NOW:

THE SPIDER

- ❏ #1: The Spider Strikes — $13.95
- ❏ #2: The Wheel of Death — $13.95
- ❏ #3: Wings of the Black Death — $13.95
- ❏ #4: City of Flaming Shadows — $13.95
- ❏ #5: Empire of Doom! — $13.95
- ❏ #6: Citadel of Hell — $13.95
- ❏ #7: The Serpent of Destruction — $13.95
- ❏ #8: The Mad Horde — $13.95
- ❏ #9: Satan's Death Blast — $13.95
- ❏ #10: The Corpse Cargo — $13.95
- ❏ #11: Prince of the Red Looters — $13.95
- ❏ #12: Reign of the Silver Terror — $13.95
- ❏ #13: Builders of the Dark Empire — $13.95
- ❏ #14: Death's Crimson Juggernaut — $13.95
- ❏ #15: The Red Death Rain — $13.95
- ❏ #16: The City Destroyer — $13.95
- ❏ #17: The Pain Emperor — $13.95
- ❏ #18: The Flame Master — $13.95
- ❏ #19: Slaves of the Crime Master — $13.95
- ❏ #20: Reign of the Death Fiddler — $13.95
- ❏ #21: Hordes of the Red Butcher — $13.95
- ❏ #22: Dragon Lord of the Underworld — $13.95
- ❏ #23: Master of the Death-Madness — $13.95
- ❏ #24: King of the Red Killers — $13.95
- ❏ #25: Overlord of the Damned — $13.95
- ❏ #26: Death Reign of the Vampire King — $13.95
- ❏ #27: Emperor of the Yellow Death — $13.95
- ❏ #28: The Mayor of Hell — $13.95
- ❏ #29: Slaves of the Murder Syndicate — $13.95
- ❏ #30: Green Globes of Death — $13.95
- ❏ #31: The Cholera King — $13.95
- ❏ #32: Slaves of the Dragon — $13.95
- ❏ #33: Legions of Madness — $12.95
- ❏ #34: Laboratory of the Damned — $12.95
- ❏ #35: Satan's Sightless Legion — $12.95
- ❏ #36: The Coming of the Terror — $12.95
- ❏ #37: The Devil's Death-Dwarfs — $12.95
- ❏ #38: City of Dreadful Night — $12.95
- ❏ #39: Reign of the Snake Men — $12.95
- ❏ #40: Dictator of the Damned — $12.95
- ❏ #41: The Mill-Town Massacres — $12.95
- ❏ #42: Satan's Workshop — $12.95
- ❏ #43: Scourge of the Yellow Fangs — $12.95
- ❏ #44: The Devil's Pawnbroker — $12.95
- ❏ #45: Voyage of the Coffin Ship — $12.95
- ❏ #46: The Man Who Ruled in Hell — $13.95
- ❏ #47: Slaves of the Black Monarch — $13.95
- ❏ #48: Machineguns Over the White House — $13.95
- ❏ #49: The City That Dared Not Eat — $13.95
- ❏ #50: Master of the Flaming Horde — $13.95
- ❏ #51: Satan's Switchboard — $13.95
- ❏ #52: Legions of the Accursed Light — $13.95
- ❏ #53: The City of Lost Men — $13.95
- ❏ #54: The Grey Horde Creeps — $13.95
- ❏ #55: City of Whispering Death — $13.95
- ❏ #56: When Thousands Slept in Hell — $13.95
- ❏ #57: Satan's Shakles — $14.95
- ❏ #58: The Emperor From Hell — $14.95
- ❏ #59: The Devil's Candlesticks — $14.95
- ❏ #60: The City That Paid to Die — $14.95
- ❏ #61: The Spider at Bay — $14.95
- ❏ #62: Scourge of the Black Legions — $14.95
- ❏ #63: The Withering Death — $14.95
- ❏ #64: Claws of the Golden Dragon — $14.95
- ❏ #65: The Song of Death — $14.95
- ❏ #66: The Silver Death Reign — $14.95
- ❏ #67: Blight of the Blazing Eye — $14.95
- ❏ #68: King of the Fleshless Legion — $14.95
- ❏ #69: Rule of the Monster Men — $16.95
- ❏ **NEW:** #70: The Spider and the Slaves of Hell — $16.95

THE WESTERN RAIDER

- ❏ #1: Guns of the Damned — $13.95
- ❏ #2: The Hawk Rides Back from Death — $13.95
- ❏ #3: Gun-Call for the Lost Legion — $13.95
- ❏ #4: The Law of Silver Trent — $13.95
- ❏ #5: The Gun-Prayer of Silver Trent — $13.95
- ❏ #6: Silver Trent Rides Alone — $13.95

G-8 AND HIS BATTLE ACES

- ❏ #1: The Bat Staffel — $13.95

CAPTAIN SATAN

- ❏ #1: The Mask of the Damned — $13.95
- ❏ #2: Parole for the Dead — $13.95
- ❏ #3: The Dead Man Express — $13.95
- ❏ #4: A Ghost Rides the Dawn — $13.95
- ❏ #5: The Ambassador From Hell — $13.95

DR. YEN SIN

- ❏ #1: Mystery of the Dragon's Shadow — $12.95
- ❏ #2: Mystery of the Golden Skull — $12.95
- ❏ #3: Mystery of the Singing Mummies — $12.95

RED FINGER

- ❏ **NEW:** #1: Second-Hand Death — $24.95